SCATTERGUN JUSTICE

The girl was hanging half out the window, one hand gripping the frame, the other waving frantically in the air. "It's a trap!" she was shouting over and over again.

Devon's attention shifted as the crack of a rifle shattered the tense stillness of the night. He caught a glimpse of Ben dashing across the street. In the confusion, a dagger of orange flame stabbed out from the corner of the building at him. Devon swung the shotgun, firing both barrels at once. Wood splintered from the corner of the building into the face of the gunman; from another direction a bullet kicked into the dust at Devon's feet.

Devon tossed the empty scattergun away and reached for the pistol at his hip—but Horschmann already had him in his sights. . . .

Also by Douglas Hirt
DEVIL'S WIND

DOUGLAS HIRT

A Passage

of Seasons

A Dell Book

Published by
Dell Publishing
a division of
Bantam Doubleday Dell Publishing Group, Inc.
666 Fifth Avenue
New York, New York 10103

All of the characters in this book are fictitious, and any resemblance to actual persons, living or dead, is purely coincidental.

ISBN: 0-440-21245-6

Reprinted by arrangement with Doubleday

Printed in the United States of America

Published simultaneously in Canada

September 1992

10 9 8 7 6 5 4 3 2 1

OPM

For Frank and Betty Roderus
my Cripple Creek connection . . . and friends

ONE

WALTER DEVON peered over the top of his newspaper at the two boys coming up the aisle. They slid into the seat across from him and, when they had settled and stowed their traveling cases, he folded the paper on his lap.

They were brothers; the younger of the two a smaller copy of the tall boy sitting next to him. They wore gray suits and starched shirts with no collars. The older boy clutched two train tickets in his hands. The younger one fidgeted in his seat and watched unhappily out the window as the train lurched and slid slowly away from the station.

Danny Medford sighed and looked away from the window, aware for the first time of Devon's dark eyes watching him. He smiled boyishly. "Mornin', sir," he said.

"Morning," Devon replied.

Brad Medford tucked the tickets into a pocket and nodded his head. "Hello," he said briefly, recalling his mother's warning about strangers. Of course, he was a man now, fully seventeen years old and traveling alone, with a ten-year-old brother to look after. Certainly he could handle anything that came his way; yet a little bit of apron string caught and held him back from pursuing the new acquaintance any further. He felt vaguely uncomfortable under the old man's gaze and blinked down at his folded hands, then dug out the train tickets again to give his fingers something to hold.

Danny studied Devon with open curiosity. His eyes riveted and expanded on the large pistol at Devon's hip and the leather holster, scuffed and worn shiny. Its stitching down at the bottom where the big-bore barrel peeked through was frayed and the leather had begun to part. The gun itself, what Danny could see of it, was mostly white metal where the bluing had worn away. Its grips were of ivory and the color of honey.

Danny noticed the other things too—the belly that folded over the belt buckle. The black wool vest that hung open except for a bottom button, which strained to keep the two halves together against the red wool bib-front shirt. His face was the color of tanned leather, etched with deep furrows like the eastern slope of the Rocky Mountains. On his head resided a brown, tattered-brimmed hat.

Danny gulped, aware of the uneasy feeling this tall, old man gave him. He saw in Devon's face the ravaging effect of years of hard living, and in Devon's nut-brown hands a trembling restlessness that made Danny think of the mountain lion he and his father had once trapped in a cage on their farm. Danny's eyes returned to the gun on Devon's hip, and he knew he'd never seen a man like him back home in Greeley. There they were all farmers. This man would be as out of place behind a plow as the men back home would be wearing a side arm and walking in two-inch-heel boots.

Even more now, Danny wished his brother hadn't taken it upon himself to veer off their intended course. He could sense nothing but trouble in it, and, with renewed unhappiness, he turned his head to the window to watch the familiar flatlands give way to the mountain slopes, as the train pulled away from the Colorado Springs Midland Terminal.

Devon sensed the uneasiness his presence had sparked in the boys and he grinned and hid his face behind the paper again.

Two hours later Danny and Brad's noses pressed against the window pane with renewed excitement. Unfamiliar landscape swept past all around them and the clatter of iron wheels against iron rails and the hypnotic sway of the coach carried them onward. Devon put away the paper and leaned back with his hat down over his eyes. He dozed, then came awake under the hat, listening to the boys talk.

"I read that there are over fifty-five thousand people living in the District," Brad was saying.

"Gosh." Danny pointed at the lingering patches of snow that clung to the north side of trees and rocks.

"Yeah, Danny. We're probably ten thousand feet high. I read where snow sometimes lingers on until July or August."

"Think there's any Indians?"

"Naw, not no more. Used to be Utes living around here, but they moved on. Mostly just miners now."

Danny looked out the window again, then heard the rustle of paper and turned back as Brad unfolded a yellowed newspaper clipping. He frowned, recalling why they had come, and said, "Brad, you think you ought to?"

A gleam flashed in Brad's eyes as he reread the paper. He glanced up. "Sure, why not? No one will know but you and me. Ma and Pa will never find out."

"But it ain't right."

"Says who?" Brad came back defensively.

Danny shrugged his small shoulders. "Anyway, what will Aunt Lucy say when we aren't on the train when it pulls into Trinidad?"

"We'll send her a telegram, telling her we got off the train in Colorado Springs and it left without us. We'll be back by morning and she won't know no difference."

Danny frowned unhappily. "I don't like lying to kin."

"You ain't gonna tell her?"

"No, Brad. I wouldn't do that to you. But I don't like it none the better."

"You worry too much, Danny. Look—" He shoved the clipping in front of Danny's face. "See, we'll have great fun."

Danny wasn't so sure. He looked back out the window. Devon yawned, removed the hat from his face and sat up, glancing out the window. "We almost there, boys?"

Brad straightened around in his seat. "Yes, sir. The conductor was by a while ago and said we'd be arriving at ten-fifty. Right on schedule."

"Ten-fifty, huh? I wonder what time it would be now?"

From an inside pocket Brad drew out a shiny, gold pocket watch. When the cover snapped open, the watch began to play "Yankee Doodle." "Ten-forty now," he said.

"That's a fancy watch you got there, son. Mind if I take a look?"

Brad hesitated, but the car was filled with other travelers. Security in numbers, Brad thought. Besides, he was all grown up now. He could handle anything that came his way if he had to, including this old man.

"Sure, it belonged to my grandfather. He gave it to me on my sixteenth birthday. Of course, that was over a year ago," Brad said, expanding his chest proudly.

"Hummmm." Devon held it to the light and let the sun flash off the polished case. The dial was white enamel with gold Roman numerals. A second hand swept around at the bottom of the face. "I'd say this is one crackerjack of a watch, son. Mighty fine." He closed the lid, then opened it again and put it to his ear as the tune played.

"It's the finest watch made," Brad said. "Says 'Elgin' right on the front."

"What's two young men like yourselves doing up here?" Devon asked.

"Going to Cripple Creek," Brad said.

"Well, I figured that's where you must be going, seeing as that's where this train is headed. Got kin there?"

"No, sir," Danny replied.

"No, we want to see the town," Brad said. "I read so much about it in *The Denver Post* that when I finally got the chance I decided to see it first hand."

"*The Denver Post*, you say. You from Denver?"

"Greeley. We got a farm there."

"That where your folks are now?"

"Yes, sir. We were going to Trinidad to spend a couple weeks with my Aunt Lucy and Uncle Bill."

"Then this is sort of a side trip for the two of you."

"That's right. I figured we could take the morning train out at two-forty and be in Trinidad by tomorrow afternoon."

Devon frowned. Cripple Creek was a raw, new town, less than nine years old and already the metropolis of the Rockies. It was a bed of sin, replete with opium dens and one-girl cribs that defied count, not to mention the more elaborate "resorts" that demanded top dollar, something the miners had plenty of these days. It was a town of goats, not a fit place for the timid sheep—and *not* a place for these two.

Brad unfurled his tattered clipping and waved it in front of Devon's nose. "See, read what *The Denver Post* says."

Devon took the paper, looked at it, then held it at arm's length and read the words. When he handed it back to the boy, he said, "Seems to describe the red-light district in some detail."

"Yeah!" Brad replied with unbridled eagerness.

Danny looked away, embarrassed.

"Looks like you boys have a big day planned."

The conductor came down the aisle, announcing that the next stop was the Bennett Avenue Station at Cripple Creek.

The boys gathered their traveling cases, then peered out the window at the imposing brick buildings shining in the mountain sunlight like new toys. Bright, red, crisp and fresh. There seemed to be hundreds of them, looking like they had been built only yesterday, which wasn't far from the truth since Cripple Creek had been nearly destroyed in the great fire of 1896. All over, new buildings were going up in a town that appeared as if it was going to grow forever. Then the train rumbled over the bridge at Poverty Gulch.

Devon unbuttoned the bottom button of his vest and tucked his shirttails into his pants. "There is where all the excitement that you boys are looking for is located," he said as they passed over the gulch.

The boys peered down at the wooden shacks that squatted under the bridge and trailed off a quarter mile down Myers Avenue.

Devon said, "Those are the one-girl cribs. Negroes up here under the bridge, the Frenchies down there at the far end. The respectable resorts begin there, and in between is anything you'd care to have."

Danny looked at Devon. He appeared taller now that he was on his feet. As the old man straightened his shirt, Danny saw the flash of something shiny pinned to it. Then the vest was buttoned over it.

"Gosh, mister, are you a sheriff?"

The old man smiled at the boy. "Marshal, son."

"Gosh."

Devon adjusted the pistol at his hip and said good-bye to the boys. He started to leave but paused and turned back. If they were his kids, he'd whip them both and send them home, he thought. But then, he reminded himself, he had no room to judge, considering how his own boy had turned out. Instead, he offered a warning and told them to be careful. He strode away down the aisle as the train hissed and shuddered to a stop.

Brad and Danny watched the big man disappear, then took their bags in hand and followed. At the station they gazed down the long avenue at the bright city that lay ahead and instantly forgot Devon's warning.

Halfway up the street Walter Devon paused and looked back at the Bennett Avenue Station. He saw the two boys in front of the station, could almost sense their excitement. They carried their leather bags down the steps and angled across the street to the sidewalk. A disquieting feeling gripped Devon as they stopped to gawk at a shop window. Well, they aren't my kids, he told himself, turning back up the street.

TWO

CRYSTAL LANE twirled a parasol over her shoulder as she strolled along Bennett Avenue. She nodded to those certain men whom she recognized and freely gave a friendly smile to the other miners who passed on the sidewalk. That was all she gave freely. At DeVere's Boutique Crystal folded the parasol and stepped through the narrow door. Out of the harsh sunlight she blinked and looked around the shop, allowing her eyes to become accustomed to the darkened interior. Grace DeVere came from the back room.

"Good morning, girlie," DeVere said, slurring her words ever so slightly.

Crystal looked away from the dusty mirror where she was patting her hair back in place and viewed Grace with disapproval in her narrowed blue eyes. She crossed the floor and leaned over the counter, hooking a finger at Grace. "Come here."

"Tsk, tsk, tsk, if you aren't my very own conscience . . . well, all right, if you must." Grace leaned close and breathed heavily in Crystal's face. "See, not a drop this morning."

Crystal pulled back and shook her head. "Then that's even worse, Grace."

"Aw, you're daffy. A little puff of the pipe now and then ain't going to hurt no one."

"It's very low class, Grace," Crystal replied.

"Look who's talking class!"

Crystal frowned and wagged her head, dislodging a long golden strand from her carefully arranged hair. "You know I'm only looking out for your well-being, Grace."

"Then why don't you come on back and join me?"

Crystal wrinkled her nose. "No! It's a filthy habit."

"Don't judge until you've tried it."

"I have no desire to smoke that stuff, thank you, Grace."

"Well, you do what you do and I'll do as I please. Speaking of what you do, I'm surprised Hazel let you sneak off."

Crystal looked back at the mirror and touched her hair softly, working the errant strand of hair back in place. "I always get mornings and afternoons off," she said. "I need to have some time to myself, after all."

"So, what are you doing here? If it's to give me a temperance lecture, you're wasting your time."

Crystal turned from the mirror, suddenly excited. "I want to buy a new dress, Grace, and a hat."

The suspicious scowl faded from Grace's flushed face. Her puffy, pink eyelids widened amiably and then she laughed. "I'm just a skeptical old crow, girlie."

"You're from Missouri," Crystal reminded her.

"Only briefly, and too many years ago for me to want to think about. What is it you got in mind?"

"Oh, I don't know. Something soft, something that fits in all the right places."

Grace grinned. "You could slip into a flour sack, girlie, and it would fit in all the right places."

"You're a dear," Crystal said, smiling, "but I don't believe a word you're saying. . . ."

"Well, believe this, girlie, if'n I had your figure, I'd still be working. . . ." Then something changed in her eyes as if a dark cloud had moved across her thoughts. "Maybe I wouldn't have had to work at all if I had going for me what you have going for you." She shrugged off the sudden somber mood and smiled with some effort. "Besides it fitting in all the right places and being soft as a baby's bottom, what else do you have in mind?"

"Peach."

Grace's eyebrows arched quizzically.

"I want something peach-colored, Grace."

She thought a minute then said, "And I know just what

you're looking for." Grace came out from behind the counter. Crystal followed her into the next room, where she opened a box on a table. "New York fashions. Just in on yesterday's train. You'll find nothing like it in Cripple Creek or anywhere else around these here parts. Not even in Denver, that I can practically guarantee you."

Crystal fondled the soft material and held it up against her, turning sideways in the tall mirror on the wall.

"It's lovely, Grace."

"And it will fit in all the right places, too. Try it on, girlie."

"Help me unbutton," Crystal said, turning her back to Grace.

Grace sighed. "I should have guessed. It's been so long since you've undressed yourself, you've forgotten how."

* * *

Karl Rheutters leaned against the brick corner of the building out of the harsh sunlight and turned a smoldering cigar slowly in his lips. He paid no attention to the bustle of people moving along the sidewalk or the traffic clotting the street behind him. Instead his eyes were turned up towards Bennett Avenue, locked on a particular brick building there. He checked his watch, and then checked it again five minutes later. Satisfied, he pushed off the brick wall and hurried across the street, dodging a trolley car and a freight wagon, and slammed aside the batwings to the Miners Exchange. He moved through the crowded barroom and slid up to the bar next to a stocky, red-haired man.

Bernard Horschmann put down the beer. "What is it, Karl?"

"I've been keeping an eye on The Old Homestead like you said. Twenty minutes ago Crystal came out the front door. She went sashaying la-de-da nice and casual up to Bennett Avenue. She's in DeVere's lady shop."

"So?"

"So, she's all alone."

"DeVere is there, ain't she?"

"That rummy? You could pop her one on the back of the

head and no one would know she wasn't drunk or done in with that stuff she smokes."

Bernard Horschmann considered that, fanning away the cloud of cigar smoke that swirled up into his face. "Naw," he decided. "I got more important things on my mind."

Rheutters laughed. "Standing here filling your belly full of beer ain't going to get your brother out of Ben Kraker's jail, is it?"

"Neither is screwing that high-priced whore."

"Yeah, but which would you rather be doing, huh?"

Horschmann drank more beer.

"Well, if you ain't interested, maybe I'll just go on over to DeVere's. . . ."

"You touch her and I'll cut you, Rheutters."

Rheutters grinned evilly. "I knew you was interested. Besides, you'll think better afterwards. Maybe then we can figure out a way to spring Harry."

"I already know how I'm gonna spring Harry. You say she's alone?"

"Was five minutes ago."

Horschmann finished his beer in a long gulp and wiped his lips with the back of his hand. "Let's get out of here."

Bernard Horschmann was German-born. He had come over when he was eight years old. His father took a job in the Pennsylvania coal mines and his mother took in laundry. His brother, Harry, was two at the time and the task of watching him fell squarely upon Bernard's shoulders.

If the coalfields taught Bernard anything at all, it was that mining wasn't the life for him. He dreamed big, but life had knocked him down at every turn. Schooling came hard and the responsibility of his brother added more of a burden. Eventually he quit school to stay home with Harry. He read books on his own, whatever he could come upon, but books were rare among the immigrant miners who had difficulty speaking the language, let alone reading it.

When his father died of the lung affliction, Bernard put the thought of schooling out of his head with a finality; book-learning was not to be his road to riches. He went down into the mines and became a number among many numbers, but he never gave up his dream of success—a dream as elusive as the fabled pot of gold at the rainbow's end.

By age twenty it had dawned on Bernard that life would never mean any more to him than fourteen hours of shoveling coal and paying scrip back to the company store. Then, slowly, a plan began to form. Life had treated him unfairly, he reckoned, and turnabout was fair play. One thought led to another, each scheme more daring than the last. He had started small, gambling for scrip with an extra ace up his sleeve. Deadly business if caught, but the exhilaration of pulling it off became addictive. At first it was all trial runs, foremost to see if it could be done, but secondly to see if his conscience was up to bearing the weight of dishonesty. To Bernard Horschmann's surprise, he was successful on both accounts.

His dream began to take on solid dimensions. The bill at the company store was paid off and his mattress began to bulge with company scrip. But Bernard knew that at this rate he'd remain only a petty cheat and thief, still trapped in a filthy company town, shoveling filthy company coal until the lung affliction killed him as it had his father, or until his crooked dealing was discovered and a rope stretched his neck. Neither one was an attractive prospect. He needed more money.

One rainy April night he got drunk. Sitting in the mud with rain drooping the brim of his hat and a bottle of whiskey in his hand, he began to form a daring plan. He looked up and saw the paymaster's shack through the sheets of rain. A light burned behind curtained windows. Bernard staggered to his feet and pressed an ear to the door. He heard no voices and rightly reckoned the paymaster was alone. Bernard tried the door. It was locked. He slid along the wall to the window and peered through a gap in the curtain. The paymaster was counting scrip into piles. Bernard's eyes bulged. He had difficulty comprehending all that money. More than he ever imagined.

He moved around back of the building and tried the door there. It opened and he slipped inside. The back room was dark. At the connecting door he heard the paymaster's soft voice counting out piles of bills. The old man never heard Bernard sneak up behind him, never knew what had killed him.

The whiskey bottle crushed his bald skull, spilling whiskey on the table and floor. In a moment of elation Bernard had never known before, he shoveled the money into a sack and started for the door. But then he stopped, looked around the little room and took several deep breaths to calm himself and make his brain think straight. If he left now, the old man's body would be found and the absence of the scrip would be apparent. He'd get caught the first time he spent a dollar more than the mine owners figured he had earned honestly. If he left now, the scrip would be worthless. No, there was a better way. Then he remembered the whiskey. The building reeked of it. Why not? he thought, and set the bottle back up on the table, spreading several hundred scrip notes on the table with it. Then he opened the lantern and sprinkled kerosene. Setting the lamp back on the table, he struck a match.

The building went up like dried tinder and by the time the fire brigade had the flames under control Bernard was safely home with a sack full of scrip and even bigger plans for the future, a future that did not include the coalfields of Pennsylvania. That night, in the quiet of his room with rain still gently drumming on the tin roof, Bernard told Harry what he had done. When Harry saw the scrip, he immediately volunteered his help in Bernard's next adventure.

Harry Horschmann, however, was not the adept thief his brother Bernard had proved to be. It wasn't too long after Bernard had taught him the technique of switching cards that a sharp-eyed miner caught Harry in the act and exposed a buried king of spades up his sleeve. They hauled him kicking and biting to the nearest hoist rigging and threw a rope over one of the beams. Harry's heels teetered on the edge of a thousand-foot shaft as they fitted the noose around his neck. About that same time Bernard, who had climbed to the roof of the hoist building, began tossing short-fused sticks of dynamite into the mob. They scattered and Bernard and Harry made it out of there with barely the clothes on their back and only what their pockets held at the time—company scrip, worthless paper anywhere but the company.

They made their way west, thinking of California and the gold and silver mines there, but then in 1891 came word of a fabulous gold strike in the mountains of Colorado. Knowing nothing but mining, the two headed for Cripple Creek with grand plans, only to discover the work was basically the same: hard, dirty and long. But Bernard already had a special talent for bilking money from honest miners and it wasn't very long before he and his brother had set themselves up in business of sorts and acquired a small gang of followers to do their dirty work for them. . . .

Bernard and Karl cut through the crowded room and out into the sunlight. At the corner Bernard suddenly grabbed Rheutters's arm and hauled him to a stop. "Damn," he hissed softly, watching the doorway across the street. Crystal Lane stepped out the front door of DeVere's Boutique with two packages in her arms, paused on the sidewalk, looked up and down Bennett Avenue as if attempting to make up her mind which way to go. She didn't care to finish her shopping with the burden of her latest purchases and, with the decision made to deposit the hat and dress back in her room, she opened the parasol and started back to The Old Homestead.

"Well, that's that," Rheutters said, turning on his heels to pursue a bottle of whiskey in the Miners Exchange, out of the sun and the heat of the late morning.

"The hell it is, Rheutters," Bernard replied. "I'm gonna get me some of that expensive pussy and I ain't gonna pay for it neither. Look, she's heading home. I think I know a place between here and there where we will be alone."

"What about Harry?" Rheutters reminded him jokingly.

"Like you said, Harry can wait. I'll think better once I get this out of my system." Bernard was suddenly aware of the fire in his blood and he knew only one remedy would cool its flames. And that remedy was strolling happily up Bennett Avenue now, thinking not of the coming evening and work, but only of the new hat and dress she'd be wearing, and the rest of the afternoon that belonged to her alone.

"Can I watch?" Rheutters asked hungrily.

A slow grin widened Bernard's face. "Sure, why not. I can teach you a trick or two. Maybe afterwards you can take a try at her."

"I thought you said you'd cut me, Bernard."

"I get real docile once I had me a woman, Karl, even generous. Come on, let's have us a time." They started back towards Myers Avenue but turned instead into an alley half-way down, moving swiftly through the shadowed brick canyons of the tall buildings.

THREE

"GOLLY!" Danny Medford said, wide-eyed. He pointed at the street that split into an upper and lower level. "Did you ever see the likes, Brad?"

"See, I told you we'd have a good time," Brad boasted.

Danny turned and pressed his nose against a window. "This town must be as big as Denver, or maybe even bigger."

"Naw, Denver is bigger." Brad pulled his little brother along the sidewalk.

"Why do you suppose they built that road that way, Brad? I mean why split it in half and lower that whole side of the town?"

"Probably had to. Probably that's the way the land lay when they built it."

"Well, I declare, you won't see nothing like that in Greeley. Brad?"

"What?"

"I'm gettin' hungry. How about you?"

The older boy opened his watch. "It's only eleven now," he said, closing the lid and burying the watch safely back in its inside pocket. They continued down the avenue, carrying their suitcases, taking in the sights. Danny stopped in front of a tall window and tried to read a poster plastered there. *Justin Tollar*. He sounded out the word below the name. *Healings*. "What's this about, Brad?"

"It's advertising a tent meeting tonight. This fellow, Tollar, is a preacher who says he can heal sick people." Brad read the poster further and pointed back towards the Midland Terminal where they had come from. In an empty lot beside it a large canvas tent flapped in the gentle breeze that came down off the mountain. "It's gonna be held over there," he said.

Danny said, "Oh," and scuffed along the wooden sidewalk after his brother. After a while they found a bench and sat down.

"Where we gonna eat, Brad?"

"I don't know."

"There's a cafe over yonder."

Brad considered the brick building with the wide window painted in gilded letters: *The Golden Cycle Cafe.* He said, "It looks expensive. How much money you got, Danny?"

Danny fished out the handkerchief his mother had tucked away safely in a pocket inside his jacket. He untied the knot and counted the coins. "Three dollars, Brad."

Brad said, "I've got three dollars and some change left. I spent five dollars for our tickets here." He thought of the possible cost of what he had planned, frowned and shook his head. "We ain't going to have enough money to go spending it on food. We'll just have to skip lunch."

Danny kicked at the sidewalk and retied the money into the handkerchief.

"If you don't think about eating you'll feel better," Brad advised.

"I ain't thinking of it, my stomach is."

"Come on, let's keep moving."

"Where to?" Danny asked, standing reluctantly, trailing after his brother.

"Down this way," Brad turned off Bennett Avenue towards the lower street a block over. At the corner Brad read the street sign. *Myers Avenue.* He unfolded the newspaper clipping and checked. "Yep, this here is the place."

"Brad?"

"What?"

Danny looked up at his older brother, then turned his eyes away and shrugged his shoulders. "I don't think this is a very good idea."

"You gettin' scared?"

"It ain't me who ought to be scared!" he replied with an air of rebellion in his voice.

"You don't have to come along. You can wait back at the depot if'n you want, but I ain't going to pass up a chance like this, no sir."

Danny shook his head. "No, Brad, I ain't gonna let you go by yourself. You might need my help."

Brad laughed. "That will be the day I need help from a tyke like you."

"I ain't no tyke!"

"Well, you certainly ain't no bruiser, neither."

"You better lay off, Brad," Danny said, tasting bile.

"Okay, forget it. You coming?"

Danny nodded his head and scuffed along behind him. They started up Myers, towards the Midland trestle where the road played out eventually in the old diggings of Poverty Gulch, where Bob Womack first discovered gold in 1890. They passed Third Street, and the fancy, new brick parlor houses gave way to the flimsy two-room, one-girl cribs. Overhead, wires sagged from pole to pole along the dusty avenue. Brad stopped once and turned back to view the direction they had come from. It might have been two different worlds, for beyond Third Street Cripple Creek seemed to be marching headlong into the twentieth century. On this side of Third time retreated.

The sun burned down on the boys, but the high-mountain air was cool and carried with it was the foul stench of human sewage. All around, clapboard buildings jostled with each other for the same piece of ground and behind them, the privies seemed to be having the same struggle. When the wind shifted the stench was almost unbearable.

The cribs had a new-old look to them as if they had been built recently, but like their hard-living occupants they aged and died quickly. Some doors hung open, others were closed. The windows were up and dingy curtains fluttered in the breeze.

"I don't like this place, Brad," Danny said cautiously.

Brad shook his head slowly. "I think maybe we should be going the other way."

A black-haired Mexican girl appeared in the doorway of one of the shacks. On the building was painted the name *Rosita*. She leaned out the door and beckoned to the boys with a wave of her hand. Danny looked at Brad, who wasn't looking at all eager at the moment. Hesitantly, he took three steps in her direction. The stench of a body unwashed overpowered him and he recoiled back a step.

"You want good time, boys?" the Mexican girl said. "I not cost much."

"No," Brad said, taking a second step backwards.

"Shush!" The Mexican girl made a emphatic move of her hand, but it was too late. Brad's startled voice had carried and now from others cribs female faces began to appear. Some poking through fluttering curtains, others stepping out the doorways in various degrees of dressed or undressedness: Kity, Franky, Lizzie, Francis, Anita, Doe, Black Molly, Elvira. The names painted on the houses identified their occupants. A dozen different girls of a dozen different countries, and they were all vying for the boys, attempting to outdo each other in lewd promises.

Brad and Danny grabbed up their bags and raced back down Myers Avenue. When they had passed Third Street, they fell against a tall, brick building to catch their breath. Up the street the girls were still calling to them and exchanging such profanities between themselves that it made Brad's face burn. He had no idea what most of them meant.

"That ain't how *The Denver Post* described it," Danny said.

"We went the wrong way," Brad replied with renewed confidence. "I should have known. Come on, let's go this way."

"You sure, Brad?"

But Brad had already started down the sidewalk. And then suddenly he stopped in front of an elegant two-story brick building and pointed. "This is it, Danny!" His excitement was hardly contained.

"What?"

"The Old Homestead! The fanciest parlor house ever! See, read what *The Denver Post* has to say." He hurriedly dug out his dog-eared clipping and thrust it in Danny's face, while his eyes gazed wondrously at the building. Danny handed it back to him unread. By this time he could recite the article by rote.

"Well, what are you gonna do, Brad?"

Brad gulped and looked at his brother, realizing for the first time that he didn't know what he intended to do. Until this moment it had been all a dream, a moment planned for carefully in his imagination, but this was suddenly reality and the clever plans and bold actions seemed remote.

"I'm . . . I'm going to go in and . . . and . . ."

"And what?"

He wanted to say, "And hire a whore," but found the words impossible to say to his little brother. Danny was embarrassed for his brother and said, "I think I'll just go on back to the depot, Brad."

"No!" Brad croaked. Now more than ever he needed someone at his side. "No, you stay."

"What will I do?"

"You . . . you can wait in the parlor. Maybe there are books or magazines with pictures or something."

"You sure?"

"Yes, I'm sure. Here, give me your money."

Danny shook his head. "But how will we get back without money?"

"Our tickets are paid for. We won't need any money at Aunt Lucy's anyway," he said, allowing a note of impatience to enter his words.

Danny hesitated, then handed the handkerchief over. Brad pushed it in his pocket. He looked at the door then back at Danny.

"Well, go on," Danny said. "If'n your mind's made up, go on and let's get it over. If there's any money left we can buy lunch and then wait at the depot for the train."

"Well . . . okay." Brad started for the door, his boots strangely heavy.

"What's wrong?"

"Nothing!" Brad glanced back irritably and stepped closer to the building, aware of the moisture beading up on his forehead and dampening his palms. He made it to the porch, stopped and hurried back.

"Now what?"

"What should I say?"

"Shoot, Brad, I don't know. You going or not?"

"You come with me. Right by my side."

"Okay."

Together they started again for that tall door, ominous now and so near. Brad's heart pounded in his chest and his ears took to ringing. He had had it all worked out. He'd gone through this very walk a hundred times in his mind. Why was it so difficult now? What was behind the door anyway that was so frightening? Women. Lots of women. Women who sold themselves a dozen times a night. They wouldn't think twice about taking his money. He told himself this and, when he climbed the stoop to the door, he reminded himself again that this was what they were there for. After all, this was Cripple Creek, not Greeley. He raised his hand to the door knob and froze. His vision went fuzzy.

"Brad?" he heard Danny inquire. He was standing on the corner again, breathing heavily and amazed to find he was not by the door anymore.

"What happened?" Brad asked, startled.

Danny shrugged his shoulders. "Don't rightly know, Brad. One minute you're turning the handle and then you heard a noise from behind the door and hightailed it away like a rabbit smelled a wolf."

Brad's lanky body fell back against the wall and slid down to the sidewalk. He planted his elbows on his knees and propped his chin in his hands.

"You okay, Brad?"

"I reckon I just ain't got the nerve," he said. "It's downright embarrassing, Danny."

Danny shoved his hands into his pockets. "Nobody saw."
"You sure?"

Danny looked around. "It appears not." He walked to the corner and glanced up Third Street towards Bennett. "Nope, nobody here neither exceptin' a lady coming down, but she's still a ways up and it ain't likely she can see over the hatbox she's a carryin'."

Well, no lady was going to see him moping around and feeling sorry for himself. He stood again, brushed his trousers and joined Danny at the corner. Danny was right. She could barely see around the hatbox to navigate the steep sidewalk. Brad gulped as she neared. She was some looker, he thought, dressed fine and twirling a lacy apricot-colored parasol over her shoulder. What was such a fine-looking lady doing coming down to this part of town, he wondered, as she paused at the mouth of an alley for her foot to feel its way cautiously off the curb.

Suddenly two men leaped from the darkened alley. Her packages went flying and she let out a scream. A hand came down and muffled it. They dragged her up a narrow gap between two buildings.

* * *

Crystal Lane recognized Bernard at once. He'd tried for her attention since her arrival in Cripple Creek almost a year ago. A dirty brute of a man who made it clear right off that he wanted what it was she had to sell but wasn't willing to pay her price. Not that he couldn't afford her. He could. But paying for her wouldn't be a conquest and Bernard needed the conquest these days.

"What do you think you're doing, Bernard?" she hissed when he dragged her to the filthy ground and released his stranglehold on her mouth.

"I'm tired of waiting, Crystal." He breathed heavily, laughing through clenched teeth. His hands stroked her body and then dug for the buttons at the back of her dress.

She struggled beneath his weight and saw Karl Rheutters's hungry look. "Get off me, Bernard!" she cried, trying to kick. But her legs were pinned.

"Feisty little bitch, ain't she, Bernard?" Rheutters said, rubbing his palms together greedily.

"Shit!" Bernard spat, having no luck with the buttons and holding her at the same time. "Take her legs, Karl," he said. "We won't bother taking it off," and he flung her dress over her head.

FOUR

BEN KRAKER cussed softly, slammed the file cabinet drawer shut and yanked out the next drawer down. He rummaged through an array of disordered papers and, not finding what he sought, slammed it shut, too. Straightening slowly, feeling the weight of his years in his bones, he looked around the office. To his back were the cells, four of them, new as the building that contained them. To his left a window looked out to the mountains and Mount Pisgah in the distance. On a rack against that wall a dozen rifles and shotguns stood at attention. To his right was a brick wall with a small window and a large map of the mining district. Scattered around the floor were four desks, his and three others shared in common with the eight constables that comprised the police force. Directly in front of him, as he stood now with his hands planted on his hips, was the door flanked by two large windows.

He looked out those windows, not really seeing the building that stood across the street. Instead, he tried to puzzle out where Chadwick Madlin had filed the court briefs to the Horschmann case. A movement outside caught his eye.

The door opened and Devon stepped in.

Ben Kraker looked up with a start, as if a ghost had just crossed his threshold. Then a wide smile replaced the look of surprise and he leaned back, grinning. "Well, I'll be damned!"

"Ben Kraker!" Devon said, coming up short in the doorway. He studied the other man's face to be certain, then laughed and thrust out a hand. "You old cow thief. What are you doing in Cripple Creek?"

They shook hands and Kraker said, "Well, come on over here and sit down. Let me look at you. How long has it been?"

Devon sat in the chair, shaking his head with surprise and delight. "Seven or eight years, I suspect. You were sheriff of Creed as I recollect, or was it Alamosa?"

"Seven years ago would make it Creed, Walt, and, if I remember correctly, you were on your way to take charge of the territorial prison in Santa Fe."

Devon nodded his head. "I worked down in the New Mexico Territory a while. Moved back up here three years ago to serve with the state penitentiary in Canon City."

Kraker looked at him soberly. "So, you're the fellow they sent to pick up that one." He jerked a thumb over his shoulder at the occupant of the nearest cell.

"Harry Horschmann, the papers say."

"That's him. Mean son of a bitch. Killed a mine manager over a card game. Holed up in a widow's home with a two-year-old baby and the woman as hostage." Kraker frowned. "Killed them both in cold blood too, from the accounts eyewitnesses gave. Matter of fact, I was just looking for the court briefs to read the particulars. The court gave him life. Hell, Walt, in the old days we'd have strung him up and saved the taxpayers from having to pay his room and board the rest of his days."

Devon gave Kraker a wry smile. "In the old days they strung up men for rustling cattle, too, Ben."

Kraker swiveled around in his seat, grinned with no humor. "I was young then, Walt."

"You were forty."

Kraker laughed. "And that was young!"

Devon smiled. "Yep, I reckon we're both relics. Look at this place. Electric trolley cars. Opera houses and fine restaurants."

"Indoor privies with running water," Kraker added.

Devon nodded. "See what I mean?"

"Telephones, too."

Devon said, "Took me two weeks of staring at one of those things before I worked up the nerve to use it. They installed one at the prison. I had the young fellows make the calls until I found myself alone with it and the weather too foul to hoof it down the street and give my message in person. I didn't even know how to make the damn thing talk to me, but kids nowadays, well, they take to them right off."

Kraker went to the stove. "A cup of coffee, Walt?"

"Sure. I was sort of expecting to find Madlin minding the store, Ben."

Kraker handed him a cup and sat back behind the desk. "You knew Chadwick?"

"Knew?" Devon asked warily.

Ben heaved in a breath and glanced at the steam rising from his coffee cup. How he hated this part of the job. "Madlin is dead."

Devon felt the warmth of the cup between his hands. "When?"

"Three weeks ago. He got between a Pinkerton man working for the mine owners and a strong arm for the WFM."

"The what?"

"Western Federation of Miners. Chad took a load of buckshot in the back. Killed him right off."

Devon contemplated the warm cup in his hands, suddenly feeling the weight of his years pressing down on him. "Chad was a good man. I knew him a lot of years. How's his wife doing?"

"Beth will make out fine. She's a strong woman. She's got her son for support, too. He's with the fire department."

Devon drew a breath, removed his hat and ran fingers through the thinning gray hair. "We all got to meet our Maker sometime, I reckon," he said soberly. "How about you, Ben? How'd you come to be here?"

"Oh, I don't know, Walt. I was sheriffing over east, in a little place called Rocky Ford. Cold country out east come winter. You wouldn't like it. I didn't. I guess growing old does that to a man. Why, back when we were young, we'd spend whole winters up north wading waist-deep through beaver water and didn't pay it no nevermind, remember?"

"I remember. Like you say, we were young then."

"I was fourteen and you were . . . how old were you, Walt?"

"I don't remember. I'm going on seventy-one come next March. You figure it."

"Well, we were both fresh-faced and ready to take life by the horns, weren't we, Walt?"

"That we were," Devon said, thinking back over the years.

"Well, anyway, that's all water under the bridge. I'm sixty-nine and I'll be retiring soon, I suspect," he said ruefully. "I was sheriffing in this eastern town when I got word Madlin had been killed. I knew Madlin, but only of recent. I sent a telegram offering my condolences and the next I knew the town of Cripple Creek was offering me the position until they could elect a new police chief. Police chief! How do you like the highfalutin sound of that title? Who'd have ever guessed when we was hunting buffalo for the Central Pacific that some day I'd be a police chief! Well, Rocky Ford needed a sheriff like Martha needed to drop a stitch. I needed a change, so I took the job."

"Who'd have thought it when you took to rounding up branded cattle down in Texas?" Devon added with a grin.

"I prefer not to think about that period of my life, Walt. Besides, you were there to bail me out and that wasn't the first time."

Devon stood and went to the windows overlooking the street. "Yep, we've had us a lot of years riding together," he said, returning to his reason for coming. "I've got the papers on that fellow back there, Ben. He fit to travel?"

"Yep, and I'll be glad to be rid of him. I knew the prison was sending someone up to fetch him, so I got the papers all signed to turn him over to you. You leaving tomorrow, or can you stay over a day or two?"

"Get him ready. I'm leaving on the two-forty morning train."

"Wish you could stay longer, but I understand."

Devon laughed briefly, "Hell, Ben, when you get as old as we are, you don't dare stand still in one place too long. Someone just might think you up and died and try to plant you."

"What are your plans between now and then?"

"Get something to eat, find a place to lay down for a couple hours."

"You're welcome to one of the cells back there."

"I'll take you up on that."

"The Merchant's Cafe is a good place to get a meal."

They relived old memories for a while and, when Devon finally left, he paused on the sidewalk and took in a deep breath of mountain air. It was good to be alive after so many years of living, good to remember the past too, he decided, but not good to remain there for very long. Tomorrow lay before him and, while he had breath in his lungs, Walter Devon would keep working for that next sunrise. To him, that was what life was all about.

He started into town, aware of an uneasiness stirring within him, an unspoken warning that he'd grown to trust, having lived most his life on the edge of danger. His shoulders tensed under the wool vest and all at once he thought about the two kids he had met on the train. What kind of trouble had they gotten into? He had no way of knowing and he shrugged off the premonition, chalking it up to an unsettled conscience on his own part. Then without warning he thought of Ferro and old feelings surfaced like an ugly wound. Thankfully, at that moment he spied the Merchant's Cafe. With a heave of resolution he locked away his feelings towards Ferro Devon and angled across the street towards the cafe. Out the corner of his eye he saw the fat man watch him from across the street. He made a mental note of it, filed it where he wouldn't forget and went inside.

* * *

At seventeen years old, Brad Medford was a tall boy, taller than most his age, and that lent an awkward appearance, which made him bow his shoulders and stoop slightly when he was with the other boys. But, when he stood proud, he topped six feet, although not yet filled out to man-size proportions.

Now he came suddenly straight, no longer concerned about his height. "Find help, Danny," he said in a voice vacant of adolescent timber and hesitation.

"But where?"

Brad Medford's searching glance landed upon The Old Homestead and he pointed. "In there." Then, knowing he had not a moment to lose, he wheeled around and into the alley into which only a few moments before he'd seen the lovely woman disappear.

Danny ran up the street and banged his fists into the front door. It opened and an elderly woman peered down at him. She smiled suddenly.

"I think you're a might too young—"

"Please, ma'am," Danny interrupted, "my brother needs help!"

Hazel Vernon saw the fright in Danny's face, put a hand on his shoulder and led him into the parlor. "Settle down, boy, settle down," she said soothingly. "Tell me what's happened."

A man on the sofa glanced away from the laughing green-eyed lady who had just poured them each a glass of wine.

Hazel Vernon calmed Danny and asked him again to explain the nature of the emergency. Danny gulped down his fear and told it all, just as they'd witnessed it. When he finished, Hazel's eyes narrowed and she said all at once, "Crystal!"

The man came off the sofa and girls were coming into the parlor from the kitchen, where Danny caught a glimpse of a table laid out with dinner. The odor of roast beef and mashed potatoes filled the room.

"Crystal is in trouble," Hazel announced. "Get on the telephone and call that new police chief—what is his name?"

"Ben Kraker," one of the girls said, disappearing back into the kitchen.

"Wait, Tom," Hazel said as the man started for the door. "Here, take this." She reached behind the kitchen door and came back with a short-barreled shotgun.

* * *

Brad had no idea what he was going to do once he caught up with them. As he pounded into the alley, he suddenly realized he had not given the consequences of his headlong action any consideration at all. He only knew that a beautiful, young lady—a girl not much older than himself—had been forcibly pulled off her course and that he was certain she desperately needed his help.

In the shadows of the building rising up around him he heard a noise and stopped. Turning, he saw movement up a narrow ravine formed by two close buildings. He saw the flash of something white in the dimness as Crystal's petticoats had been flung over her head and he swallowed hard, aware of his own fear catching up with him.

They were men. Vicious men, obviously, and what could he do to stop them? Yet everything in Brad's being told him he must stop them! Fighting down his fears, he pulled himself up straight and, with determination in his voice, he said, "Hey, you two! What are you doing?"

Bernard Horschmann spun around and saw the tall, dark silhouette blocking the light at the end of the buildings.

"Oh, shit!" Rheutters said softly.

Bernard stood. "Get out of here, mister, this is none of your affair."

"Let the girl go and I'll leave." Brad's voice faltered.

Bernard glanced at Rheutters and a smile inched up the corners of his lips. "He's only a kid. Hold her, Karl." A stream of sunlight through the dimness above flickered off the boot knife that appeared in Bernard's hand.

Brad backed out into the alley, trying desperately to recall what he knew about fighting, which had never been very much. Bernard neared and Brad's eyes widened on the knife in the man's hand.

"I'll teach you about poking your nose where it don't belong," Horschmann said, waving the blade in a smooth, deadly arch.

"Just . . . just let the girl go." Brad tried and failed to get a grip on the emotion that showed itself in his voice.

"Why? Because you say so?" Bernard lunged.

Brad expected that and sidestepped. He swung at the knife hand, missed and regained his balance a moment before the knife sliced empty air in front of his face. Horschmann lunged again and Brad suddenly had a cold, brick wall at his back. An evil glint came to Horschmann's eye. He had the meddling kid now. A quick thrust and he could get back to the girl. . . .

The roar of a gun thundered down the alley. Brad slipped around him and knocked the knife from Bernard's hand in that moment, as the man at the end of the alley leveled the shotgun.

"I'll take care of you later!" Horschmann said and fled. Rheutters peered around the corner, saw a man, several women and a young boy coming towards him and took off after Bernard.

Danny ran to Brad. "Are you all right?"

"Yeah, I think so."

"Where is Crystal?" Hazel demanded.

Brad pointed at the gap and at that moment Crystal Lane appeared. She looked disoriented. Hazel put an arm around the girl and, after she assured herself that Crystal was uninjured, they all left the gloom of the alley. Brad gathered up Crystal's packages from the gutter and carried them for her.

His mind was still in a whirl, his heartbeat and breathing were rapid and now, as he followed the procession down Myers Avenue, he was aware of the sweat under his chin and the sudden shiver that made him shake uncontrollably. He managed to fight it down. No one noticed. He clamped his eyes shut, opened them again and didn't even realize until the door closed behind him that he had entered The Old Homestead.

FIVE

CRYSTAL LANE came down the stairs a few minutes later with no trace of the attack remaining. Her damaged dress had been exchanged for the new one she'd just purchased from Grace DeVere and her pink cheeks had a clean, scrubbed and powdered look about them.

Hazel Vernon was waiting in the parlor. She smiled when she saw Crystal descending the stairs, turned to Ben Kraker and said, "Here she is now."

"Ma'am," Kraker said politely, stepping in front of the staircase.

"This is Police Chief Kraker, dear," Hazel said.

"Yes?"

"Would you care to tell me just what happened, Miss Lane?" Kraker stepped aside as she dismounted the stairs and moved past in a graceful swirl of apricot lace, leaving behind the lingering scent of perfume. She peered out the front window at Myers Avenue, her back towards the room.

"His name is Bernard Horschmann," she said. "He has been bothering me for months. I don't know his friend's name, although I have seen them together. Mostly they spend time at the Miners Exchange."

Horschmann? Kraker thought of the younger Horschmann locked up in a cell back in his office. He'd heard of the brother, Bernard, in the few weeks he had been in town. He had been warned the older brother might make an attempt to free Harry. The stories circulated describing Bernard as the devil's own kin, but he watched over Harry with a devotion that bordered on fanaticism. Kraker recalled hearing how Bernard had snatched his brother from a lynch mob in Pennsylvania, and figured he'd try the same here in Cripple Creek. The fact that he hadn't made a move yet on the jail had Kraker concerned. Now that Walt Devon was here to take him, Kraker figured a time of confrontation was drawing near.

"Were you injured, ma'am?"

She turned. "No. I am quite all right, thanks to that young man." She nodded and smiled at Brad.

Brad felt his cheeks begin to burn. Kraker looked at the boy sitting nervously on the sofa and said, "What's your name, son?"

"Brad, sir. Brad Medford."

"You didn't get hurt?"

"No, sir."

"You from around here?"

"No. We're from Greeley."

Kraker indicated Danny with a nod. "Your brother?"

"Yes."

"Your folks in town, son?"

Brad's eyes suddenly widened. Would this be reported to his parents? He shrank back under the older man's gaze and shook his head. "No, sir . . . they're . . . they're . . . they're both dead, sir." Instantly he regretted the lie.

Danny's head came about with a jerk and a look of surprise, but he didn't deny the statement.

Brad was certain now that the police chief had seen the lie.

But Ben Kraker had more immediate problems than looking for an untruth in the boy's statement. "I'm sorry to hear that, son," he said briefly, then added, "you two best keep your eyes open. Cripple Creek is not a forgiving town and Myers Avenue isn't a street to be playing on."

"Yes, sir," Brad said, recalling a similar warning given to them by another old man. "We was just passing through. We will be leaving on the morning train."

Kraker returned his attention to Crystal Lane. "I reckon you want to swear out a complaint?"

Crystal shook her head. "I don't think so."

Kraker frowned. A complaint was what he desperately needed. With Bernard Horschmann behind bars, he could eliminate the worry of an escape attempt. But free, no telling when the man might strike. "Are you certain?" he persisted. "A man like that ought to be locked away, and without your signed complaint I'd have no legal justification for doing that."

She shook her head. "No, I think not. I'm sorry."

"Might I ask why?"

"The reason is quite simple," she replied gently. "Horschmann has lots of friends in town. Men friends. Dangerous friends." She lowered her eyes, then looked up again with a reconciled smile on her face. "I see a lot of men, let's face it. Any one of them could be sent by Horschmann if my complaint sends him to jail. I can't take that chance."

"I understand," Kraker said ruefully. "Then you don't need me anymore. We'll be going." He hesitated a moment longer, hoping that she would change her mind. But, seeing the look of resolve that hardened her face, he nodded at the uniformed constable who had been standing silently aside and they went out the door.

Hazel went to Crystal. "You did the right thing, honey."

"I'm not so sure." Crystal looked sad but regrouped and spread a smile across her face. "I haven't had a chance to thank you," she said to Brad.

It had taken him a while to comprehend all that had occurred in the last half hour and only now did Brad begin to look around himself, in awe, at his surroundings. Only of late did he fully realize that the lovely young girl he had rescued was a . . . He had difficulty associating Crystal Lane with the word, but it was plain she lived here and knew the other girls. She was a whore. Well, perhaps that was too harsh a word. What was it *The Denver Post* had called them? Painted ladies?

"Yes, ma'am," he replied in a softly awed voice.

Crystal looked at Danny. He was squirming on the thick sofa and glancing hungrily at the kitchen door, where the rich odors of a fancy dinner drifted into the parlor. She glanced at Hazel Vernon. Hazel understood and nodded in reply.

"You two look hungry. Please stay for dinner."

"Yes, ma'am!" Danny said at once. Brad couldn't believe his good fortune. Here he was, so close to his goal! Inside The Old Homestead, being favored by one of the prettiest girls he'd ever seen, and she was a "painted lady" to boot!

"We'd be honored to stay," he said.

"Well, that will be just fine," Hazel said. "We were just fixing to eat when this all started. Tom was going to join us, too, weren't you, Tom?"

He shifted his gaze momentarily from his green-eyed lovely and gave Hazel a nod of his head.

"Well, then, let's get started." Hazel ushered them all into the kitchen, which also served as a dining room, and directed each to their seats. The girls already knew where they belonged and they moved in an extra chair to fill out the required number.

Danny dug into the food without a second thought. Brad was getting used to the idea of where he was, but now he had a problem. How did one go about hiring a girl? He already knew which one he wanted, for throughout dinner he hardly let his eyes wander from Crystal, and she was not oblivious to his attentions either.

Crystal was nineteen and had come to the mining camp a year earlier from a brief but painful stay in the tenderloin district of Leadville. She carried the marks of a drunken miner who decided she had paid too much attention to another man. Crystal got away lucky. The sandy-haired boy she had been seeing had not been so lucky. The miner was hanged for murder and when Crystal recovered from her wounds she traveled down to Cripple Creek vowing to find a high-class resort that catered to a different breed of men. She found the place in The Old Homestead and Hazel Vernon treated her and the other girls as if they were all her own daughters.

Crystal smiled at Brad, instinctively knowing what the boy

wanted. Brad reddened and looked down at the mound of food on his plate. He wasn't a bad-looking boy, she decided, eyeing him professionally, as a butcher might eye a side of beef. And she figured she owed him at least that.

Why did he look away? he wondered, scolding himself for his timidity. After all, she was what he wanted. He was a man, full-grown and looking out for a kid brother. Wasn't it about time he began to act like a man? Still, he couldn't bring himself to look her fully and purposefully in the eye. Instead he managed a glancing look and asked if she would please pass the mashed potatoes, which happened to be at her elbow. He reddened when he realized he already had a mound of potatoes on his plate and proceeded to add to the mound.

A wooden box on the wall suddenly rang. One of the girls went to it, put a black cone to her ear and talked at the box. Danny's fork drooped from his fingers as his mouth gaped and his eyes widened. Apparently the box was talking back. In a moment the girl returned and said, "Lisa has an appointment for tonight."

"What time?" Lisa asked, pushing back her chair.

"Eight-thirty."

She went to a chalkboard that hung on the wall and scribbled in the time behind her name. "Who was it?" she asked.

"Tab Lorimer."

Lisa turned back with a frown. "Oh, him," she said. "Why do I always get the strange ones?" She sat back at the table. There followed some giggling and brief descriptions of other strange men the girls had known. Hazel Vernon clapped her hands together and told them that dinner was not a place to talk shop, especially when there were guests present, and she nodded at Danny.

Hazel said, "I lost my folks when I wasn't much older than you, Brad. What did your folks die of?"

Brad swallowed hard and glanced at Danny, who wasn't offering any help. "Ah . . ." he paused, "they died from Injuns, ma'am."

"Indians?" Hazel looked at the boy then said, "What kind

of Indian problem are they having out Greeley way—you did say you two was from Greeley?"

"Yes, ma'am. We had a little farm there. But the Injuns burned us out, they did, and then afterwards the neighbors sent us on our way to our Aunt Lucy in Trinidad."

"I see," Hazel said.

"That sounds simply terrible," Crystal added.

Tom glanced at his green-eyed friend and struggled with a grin. Hazel swallowed back a smile and saw the confused look on Lisa's face.

"Well, what's bothering you, girl?" she asked.

"I ain't never heard o' no hostile Injuns in these parts of late," Lisa said blankly.

"That's because there ain't none!" Hazel replied. "They must have been reservation Indians. Ain't that right, Brad? They was reservation Indians that killed your folks. They probably got liquored up and slipped off the reservation and did the terrible deed."

Now even Lisa had picked up on it. Brad nodded his head. "Yep, that's what they was, all right. Reservation Injuns."

"Well, you two were lucky to get away with your scalps," Tom said, trying to keep a straight face.

Danny didn't look around and kept his dismay hidden by paying strict attention to the mound of food on his plate. He didn't much care for telling lies, especially when they got out of hand as this one had. Just the same, Brad was his brother and he was duty-bound to defend him if the occasion should occur.

Hazel Vernon said, "Well, boy, if'n your Aunt Lucy is down in Trinidad what are you and your brother doing here in Cripple Creek?"

How could he say it? The words caught in his throat and now he knew for sure his face was going to give away his true intentions. Thankfully, Crystal came to his rescue.

"I think Brad has come to Cripple Creek to visit us, Hazel."

One of the girls chuckled and then choked it back at Crystal's pointed stare.

Brad thought Crystal had put it quite delicately and wished he had said it.

"Is Crystal right?" Hazel asked.

After an embarrassing moment Brad nodded his head. "Yes, ma'am," he said, his voice barely above a whisper.

Mary Towers hid a smile behind her napkin.

Tom and his green-eyed beauty exchanged guarded grins. Hazel considered him a few seconds then nodded her head.

"Well, I reckon you're old enough, what with your folks gone and you in charge now."

Suddenly the embarrassment passed and again Brad was in control. With renewed eagerness, he said, "Yes, ma'am, I reckon I am."

"Well, which one of my girls do you want?"

Brad recalled a cattle auction he had once attended with his father. Somehow it came vividly to mind now. Instinctively, he touched the pocket that contained the dog-eared newspaper clipping. All his planning was finally going to work out, perhaps not exactly as he had imagined it—and he had imagined it a hundred different ways—but it was all going to come together in the end. He could not contain his victorious smile. Now Danny felt his own face growing hot.

"I want Miss Crystal, ma'am."

"*Miss* Crystal," one of the girls said with special emphasis, but Brad was too pleased with himself to hear.

"Well, I think we can work that out." Hazel leaned back and studied the chalkboard. "Crystal should be free by nine o'clock, Brad, if you can wait that long."

"Oh, I can wait!" He glanced at Crystal, pleased to see her smiling eagerly back at him.

"Then it's all settled." Hazel turned back to the table with a half-smile on her face. "Crystal will cost you forty dollars."

Brad's jubilant face went limp. His mouth parted heavily. "Forty dollars!"

"That's what my girls cost, Brad," Hazel replied.

Crystal said, "Considering how Brad helped me this morning, Hazel, perhaps we could make an exception?"

Brad's face brightened.

Hazel said, "I certainly appreciate it when someone helps one of my girls and, to show my appreciation, I've given them both a sizable dinner and they've eaten well of it, my dear. But business *is* business, after all."

Crystal looked at Brad and heaved her shoulders helplessly. "I tried, Brad."

"But I ain't got that much," Brad said desperately.

"How much have you?"

"All I got is six dollars."

"Six dollars will be enough up the street," Tom said. "Matter of fact, six dollars would do you two or three times."

The notion was repulsive. There was no comparing the filth and stench of the one-girl cribs up the street to the clean elegance of The Old Homestead. He shook his head convulsively. "No!"

Hazel smiled gently. "Well, I do appreciate you thinking of us, Brad, and if you ever get back this way with more cash in your pocket please stop in again."

He was too close to victory to let Crystal slip away from him like the vapor of a dream—an unfulfilled dream. Here he was in Cripple Creek! The City in the Rockies! All his planning, the money already spent, his goal, lovelier than he ever imagined, sitting across the table from him. He was seventeen years old already and he had never had a woman. Maybe he never would if he let this opportunity slip away. No, he couldn't! He'd get the money even if he had to steal it! Brad reeled at that thought. Well, perhaps he wouldn't steal it, but he knew he could raise it somehow. "No!" he said suddenly. "I'll get the money."

"But how, Brad?" Crystal asked.

"I . . . I don't know, but I will. You just save me that time at nine o'clock and I'll be back."

Danny didn't like the sound of that, as he played with his food, his appetite suddenly gone.

SIX

THE FOOD at the Merchant's Cafe was satisfying and, with the hole in the pit of his stomach filled, Walter Devon leaned back comfortably in his chair to enjoy a second cup of coffee. The sun had climbed high in the sky and burned down through the thin, mountain air. Beyond the windows of the Merchant's Cafe, it cut sharp, narrow shadows against the tall buildings. As he studied the people moving along the sidewalk, he was aware of a lingering uneasiness that the good food and pleasant surroundings hadn't fully dispelled. With a sudden frown he finished his coffee, paid the bill and went outside.

Devon spied the source of his uneasiness immediately. The fat man he'd noticed a few moments before he had entered the cafe was still there. His position had shifted from the front of the big Van Camp's Beans advertisement painted on the side of the Howard Building to an inconspicuous location up the street in a doorway. Devon tugged his hat down to shade his eyes and started up the street. As he passed the doorway, he glanced in.

The heavyset man looked hot under a dark, wool jacket. His head was bald and beaded with sweat. He hadn't been out of the sun very long, Devon decided, as he strolled past him. He had probably been somewhere near the Merchant's Cafe, watching Devon through the windows. Now the fat man appeared intent on the handbill he was reading. Devon saw the bulge under the coat at the waist. A bulge that wasn't part of the fat that strained the buttons of the coat.

It might be nothing, an innocent coincidence. But his gut

feeling said no. Devon continued on and turned up a side street. At the Imperial Hotel he paused to read a menu posted in the window. The fat man stopped at the corner and peered off in another direction. Devon smiled to himself, certain now, and continued up the hill towards the residential section of town.

Devon passed a Catholic Church, wheeled about abruptly and went up the steps. In the narthex he moved up near a narrow window. The fat man lingered two houses down, breathing heavily from the climb up from town. He unbuttoned his coat now and sleeved the sweat from his brow. The coat parted and the sun glinted off a nickel-plated revolver tucked in his waist band.

Suddenly Devon was aware of someone behind him.

He spun around, his hand moving, then stopped and drew in a deep breath and let it out slowly, looking into the startled eyes of a priest.

The priest's eyes narrowed sharply. His voice remained level but firm. "Can I help you?" he asked, suspecting that the kind of man Devon was put him beyond the church's ability to help.

Devon, drawing to his full height, smiled pleasantly at the man. "If you just show me the back door, padre, I'll be leaving."

"God's house is not a public thoroughfare, sir, and certainly no place for guns." He glanced at Devon's holstered pistol and then peered beyond him and out the window at the fat man. He looked narrowly back to Devon's face. "Are you running from that man out there?"

"I never ran from any man, padre, including that yahoo out there. God's house may become a slaughterhouse unless you show me the back door." He peeled back his vest and showed the tin star pinned on his shirt.

Something changed in the priest's face. "I see, marshal. I didn't realize you were a lawman. Certainly you can use the back door and . . ."

"Thank you, padre," Devon said, cutting short the offer of help he knew was coming. He followed the priest through the church, paused a moment as the priest genuflected in front of the alter, then stepped out a door the priest held open for him. Down the back steps he checked his bearings, crossed a backyard and moved along the side of the house.

* * *

Boyd Rawlin had seen Devon go up the steps of the church and waited, wiping the sweat from his eyes. After a few minutes he checked the time. He pushed the watch back into a vest pocket, wondering what business Ben Kraker's friend had in a church.

He leaned against a wrought iron fence. He stiffened and his heart skipped. He inhaled sharply and his flaccid body began to quiver. The cold steel of a gun barrel jabbed his thick neck. A hand reached around him and removed the pistol from his belt.

"Any more hardware?" a voice behind him asked.

Boyd shook his head.

"Turn around, real slow, and keep your hands where I can see them." The gun Devon had taken from him was a Forehand & Wadsworth .38. He tucked it into his belt.

"You've been following me, mister. I want to know why."

"You've made a mistake," Boyd Rawlin stammered. He'd only seen Devon from afar. Now, up close, he shrank back from the bulk of the wide shoulders and from the craggy face, hard as old leather, that peered down at him.

"You waited for me outside the cafe and followed me up here. I want to know why."

Boyd's brown eyes blinked in their fleshy lids, then narrowed at the glint of metal pinned to Devon's shirt.

"You . . . you're a lawman?"

"That's right."

"Honest, sir," Boyd stammered, "I was just out walking. I ain't never seen you before. Why would I want to follow you?"

"I don't know. That makes me real suspicious. And you toting a concealed pistol in your belt." But Devon had no hard evidence except his gut feeling. He couldn't rail the man on that, no matter how certain he was of its validity.

This was 1899, after all, not 1870. The West was civilized by the pile of laws fresh-faced Eastern lawyers wrote to hog-tie a lawman's hands and give free rein to criminals.

"All right, get out of here. But be warned, if I see your face again, I'll run you in on disturbing the peace." Devon tapped himself with his thumb. "My peace."

"Yes, sir. You won't be seeing me again. Ah . . . could I have my gun back?"

"And that's another thing. I'll run you in for carrying a concealed weapon. I'm sure Cripple Creek has an ordinance against it; I'll be checking to see. If you want your gun back, you can pick it up at Ben Kraker's office."

"Yes, sir." Boyd was anxious to get away, even at the cost of a seven-dollar pistol. He hurried down the street back into town. Devon stood there until Boyd had disappeared. He holstered his gun and strolled back to Ben Kraker's office.

* * *

Kraker looked up from a mess of papers on his desk. "How was dinner?"

Devon dropped Boyd's pistol on the desk. "I took that off some yahoo who was following me. I told him he could claim it here, but I wouldn't put any money that he'll ever come for it."

"Where is he now?"

Devon shrugged his shoulders. "I don't know. He high-tailed it back into town. Didn't bother to ask his name. Short, heavy fellow who ought to eat less and exercise more."

Kraker's forehead furrowed. "I don't like that."

"Worried about your prisoner back there?"

"I suspect his brother is going to try something."

"You hear anything definite?"

Kraker shook his head. "No, nothing for sure. But word is, Bernard Horschmann looks after his little brother like a compulsive mother hen. I can't believe he'll let Harry be carted off to prison without a try."

"You better believe that," Harry Horschmann said from his jail cell.

Devon glanced up. Horschmann leaned against the bars, grinning. His face wore the beginnings of a beard and his hair needed combing. "Tell you truthfully, I didn't expect to be here as long as I have. But I ain't worried. Bernie will get me out."

"Don't bet money on that, fellow."

"How is an old man like you figuring on stopping Bernie? My brother will eat you up and spit you out in little pieces."

Devon allowed himself a shadow of a smile. It went unnoticed by Harry but not by Kraker, who'd seen that look a time or two before. Once when they were boys up in Montana and a Blackfoot hunting party appeared suddenly across their trail. Their mules were loaded with a winter's catch and the Indians wanted the beaver they carried. And another time down in West Texas when a group of irate cattlemen had a rope around Kraker's neck. Devon had come down out of the hills with a sawed-off Purdy double shotgun over his arm and that same shadow of a smile upon his face. Both times Devon had come out of the spat on top.

But now Kraker was troubled. They were both old men; Kraker felt it more, but that didn't mean age hadn't slowed Devon down, too, hadn't weakened his muscles and sapped the endurance Devon had relied on so often to tip the battle in his favor. Now the challenging smile that appeared and passed made Kraker wish the prison had sent another man to transport Harry Horschmann.

Devon turned back, immediately aware of the troubled look on Kraker's face, and he knew what had put it there. "Ben, don't pay that gunsel's words no nevermind. He's making brave, 'cause deep down inside he's about ready to pee in his pants."

Harry threw the tin water cup at Devon, missed and the cup clattered against the far wall. Devon picked up the cup and returned it to Horschmann. Moving swiftly he snatched the younger man's arm and yanked him to the bars. "Let's get one thing straight from the start, mister. I'm taking you in and if that don't sit easy with you keep it to yourself. The next time you throw a cup or anything else, you'll be picking bits and pieces of it from your teeth. You can arrive in Canon City all in one piece, or you can arrive bloody. It makes no difference to me."

Devon held him there against the bars while their eyes locked. Horschmann finally blinked away and when he did Devon pushed him back into the cell and dropped the tin cup in after him.

"You can't treat me like that, marshal."

"I just did."

"You think you made an impression?" Kraker asked softly.

Devon sat in a chair with his back to Horschmann. "You can't buffalo men like him. I meant it and he knows it. Trouble is, he doesn't believe I can stand good on the threat. He'll have to find out for himself."

"I don't like this, Walt."

Devon laughed. "You've taken to worrying more than I remember, Ben. They say that gives a man indigestion. We're too old for that kind of nonsense, you and I."

"Maybe, Walt. Just the same, I don't like the feel of it. It's reminding me of Texas. . . ."

"And we made it out of that one all right."

"By the skin of our teeth."

Devon stood. "Well, we still have some of that skin left, don't forget. I'm going to take me a little nap, Ben. Got a long night ahead. Which one of these fancy new cells you want me to bunk down in?"

Kraker waved a hand. "Take your choice. When you want me to wake you?"

"Give me a couple hours. Wake me at six if I'm not already stirring."

SEVEN

BRAD MEDFORD sulked by the corner street lamp, eye-ing The Old Homestead and trying to plan his next move. Danny paced in a circle, his hands thrust deep into the pockets of his trousers, an impatient look on his smooth face.

"You ought to forget it, Brad. It ain't workin' out and there ain't no way you're gonna get your hands on forty dollars 'tween now and nine tonight."

"Yes, I will. You can wait up to the depot for me. I'll do it alone."

"No . . . no, I'll stick with you, Brad."

Brad looked at him mockingly. "In case I need help? You saw how I handled those two who wanted to harm Miss Crystal. I can take care of myself. Go on. Get, if you want."

Danny just shook his head and leaned against a lamp post. "I'll stay."

"Then help me figure out a way to—" He stopped suddenly and looked down Myers Avenue. His face brightened. "I got it. Come on."

Danny didn't like the sound of that, but all he could do was follow. Brad stopped on the sidewalk outside the Golden Charm Saloon and peered over the batwings into the dark, smoky room.

"What you plannin', Brad?"

He glanced back eagerly. "I'm gonna win us the money. I'll just sit in on a card game and when I've won the forty dollars I need I'll quit."

"But you can't play poker, Brad!"

"Can too. I played it lots o' times with Uncle Jethro back

behind the corn crib. And a few times with Larry Waters after school."

"But that weren't real cardplaying," Danny objected.

"Real enough. And I usually won, too."

"But we ain't got no money."

"Got six dollars."

"You might lose it all."

"Won't either. Give me your share."

Danny shoved a reluctant hand into his pocket and came out with the knotted handkerchief. He recalled their mother's care in preparing for their trip. Her searching the bottom of her cookie jar for the coins and then wrapping them tightly, tying them in place with a sturdy knot and solemnly handing each of them the small bundles, saying it was for emergencies. Danny felt a deep guilt giving it to Brad to gamble with for more money to buy favors from the pretty lady at The Old Homestead. At ten years of age, Danny wasn't quite sure what the fuss and urgency was all about. If it was up to him, he'd rather spend it at the ice cream parlor he'd spied on Bennett Avenue.

"Well?" Brad asked.

Danny frowned and handed it over. Brad unknotted the handkerchief and palmed the coins. "Now, you wait right here. It ain't proper for a kid to go in."

Danny protested, but Brad had already pushed through the doors. He peeked under the batwings and watched Brad inch nervously up to a table with an empty chair and three men tossing around cards. Danny expected trouble at any moment, but instead one of the men motioned to the chair and Brad slid into it, stacking his money on the table.

Brad glanced at the door, saw Danny's face under the batwings, then turned his attention to the three whiskered and craggy faces that watched him, buzzardlike, as he counted out his six dollars.

Ernest Schohn was a straw boss for the Portland mine, a man approaching forty years of age, but hard work made him appear closer to fifty; gray hair, inherited from his mother's side, lent credence to the impression. He watched

Brad stack his money and said, "Five-card draw, dollar ante. Any questions?"

"No."

Schohn dealt the cards. George Ferl, the ferrier, held them close to his vest. Malcolm Hollendorfer collected them with his right hand keeping the stump of his left hand below the table. His one good eye glanced at Brad, then back at the cards. He fumbled to spread them apart.

Brad reminded himself that bluffing was part of the game and tried to keep his feelings from showing on his face.

"I'm in for a dollar," Hollendorfer said, pushing the coin across the table with his stump. He'd been a hoist operator for the Cash-On-Delivery Mine when a cable snapped and severed his hand and put out his eye at the same time. The owner of the C.O.D., Spenser Penrose, kept Hollendorfer on in the recording house, where he tallied the carloads of crushed rock brought out of the mine.

Ferl pursed his lips, looked at his cards and decided the hand wasn't worth it. "I pass."

Brad had a mixed hand; seven, three, five, ace and a queen, but he'd already anted in a dollar. He couldn't afford to let it go without a try. "I'm in," he said, adding his dollar to the bet.

Ernest Schohn saw the bet and, when it went around again, Hollendorfer asked for three cards.

Brad swallowed heavily when it came to his move. He had two dollars staked. He knew his concern showed, but that couldn't be helped. He called for two cards, discarding his three and the five. They slid across the table to him and he filed them into his hand. He got a three back, and a seven! A pair of sevens now. If he only had discarded something other than the three he'd be sitting comfortably with two pairs. Still, it was better than he'd started with. A smile tugged at the corners of his lips.

Schohn saw the smile flicker and pass on Brad's face, knew his own hand was meager and folded. Hollendorfer laughed. "Looks like it's jest me and you, boy."

Brad nodded.

"I'm willing to stake another dollar you ain't got nothin' there."

Brad had no choice. He saw the bet. Three dollars gone. He'd likely never be able to finish a second game if he lost. Then, hardly aware of his own words, he heard himself raise the bet another dollar and pushed the coin into the pot.

Hollendorfer narrowed his good eye at Brad. The gray beard shifted with his chin. "You're lookin' scared, boy. I think I'll just see your raise. What you got?" he said.

"Pair of sevens."

"Well, I'll be damned. You had it after all!" And he tossed his cards to the table showing the pair of sixes.

Schohn laughed. "Serves you right, Malcolm, betting on a pair of sixes."

"I thought the kid was bluffing."

"You mean I won?"

"Take the pot, boy," George Ferl said.

Brad pulled the coins to his corner and counted out ten dollars. With the two dollars he still had, he was well on his way to firming up his appointment with Crystal.

The cards fell smartly for Brad the next three hands and, with a new lady friend named Luck looking over his shoulder, he won them in such rapid succession it made him giddy.

As Ferl gathered in the cards, Brad counted his winnings. He'd never seen forty dollars all together in one place before. Forty dollars! And there was more. He made a third pile of the the smaller coins that remained in his hot palm. Altogether, it amounted to forty-six dollars. Enough to meet his appointment with Crystal and still have some left over to buy a meal for Danny and himself afterwards. Yep, he thought, it was all going to work out after all. He felt suddenly good about coming to Cripple Creek, as if this winning had confirmed his right to claim manhood for his very own. He was indeed in control of his own destiny! But such euphoria can be numbing to the senses and, as he gathered in his winnings, Brad was unaware of the five eyes that watched him from around the table.

Brad dropped the coins into his pocket. He started to stand when Schohn's hand came down upon his wrist in a viselike grip. "Where do you think you're going, boy?"

The suddenness of it all confused Brad and stripped away his momentary lapse into euphoria. "I . . . I've got to leave now."

Hollendorfer scratched an itch under the black eye patch. "You just won a lot of money off of us, boy. You can't up and leave on us. That ain't the way it's done." His voice was low and threatening.

A lump blocked Brad's throat. "But I need to go now. My little brother is waiting for me and—"

"Sit back down," Schohn said.

A momentary urge to flee came over him, but Schohn's hand was still clamped to his wrist.

George Ferl said, "Let the kid go, Ernest. He's still wet behind the ears."

"Not till I get a chance to win back my money."

"He won it off you fair."

Hollendorfer waved his stump at Brad and said to Ferl, "That ain't the point, George. The point is, we let this kid sit in on our game and it ain't proper he should skedaddle off, carrying with him the luck of the first few hands. Ernest is right. We ought to have another chance at him. Two more hands and the kid can go."

Ferl agreed to that.

Schohn looked at the boy. "You heard it. Two more hands." Brad glanced at Danny's pink face under the batwings and reluctantly returned to his chair. He piled the money up in two small stacks and his stomach knotted as the cards came around.

Brad fanned them out in his fingers and placed two eights side by side. A three, a king and an ace remained. Ferl opened the bet with a dollar and it was called all around. Brad discarded the three and king, received a two and five in exchange. His suits were mixed and against his better judgment he called the next raise. The first hand he had won with a pair of sevens. This time he had a pair of eights. He lost three dollars to George Ferl, who laid down a pair of threes and a pair of fives. Schohn had a pair of kings and Hollendorfer ended with five unmatched cards.

The cards came to Brad and he shuffled them and Ferl cut the deck. Calming a shaking hand, he dealt the cards in a circle and put the remaining deck at his side. When the cards bloomed in his fingers, two jacks presented themselves. Brad arranged his face, he hoped, with no expression at all and waited for Schohn to open the bet. It was predictable, and a dollar went into the pot from each of their piles.

Feeling confident, Brad raised the bet when it came his turn. Ferl, always a cautious player, folded. Schohn pondered his hand, then called Brad's raise. Hollendorfer called, too. Schohn asked for two cards. Hollendorfer asked for one and Brad took three and held his breath as he turned over a king and a pair of twos.

Schohn checked. Hollendorfer bet a dollar and both Brad and Schohn called. Schohn laid out a pair of fours and saw right away the grin spread across Hollendorfer's face. Brad swallowed back his fears as Hollendorfer turned up a pair of twos and a pair of tens, then smiled as he showed his twos and jacks.

"I'll be damned. The kid did it to us agin," Hollendorfer said.

"You should have let him leave when he wanted to," Ferl commented.

"Run off, boy," Schohn said.

Brad looked at the mounting money. More money than he had ever imagined owning. "I'll stick for one more hand," he said confidently.

Schohn dealt it and Brad lost ten dollars in a careless gesture of bravado when Hollendorfer raised and raised again. But he was still far ahead and he decided to stick for one more hand and bet conservatively.

Hollendorfer allowed Ferl to shuffle for him and Schohn to cut. He dealt them out one-handedly. No one seemed interested in losing much money and it went around first with a series of checks and then each putting in a dollar apiece. Brad's pair of threes were topped by Hollendorfer's fives.

Brad studied the stack of coins in front of him and weighed his next move. Out the corner of his eye he saw Danny's anxious face. One more time, he decided, knowing he could win back a couple of dollars, even though he had more than enough before him to see his plans through. But that wasn't the full point of it now. He was a man, full-grown and in control of his own destiny, and this was what he wanted to do. The bug had bitten him and it was going to take at least one more hand for Brad to shed the venom of gambling fever from his system.

Ferl dealt Brad three aces, a king and a four. Brad steeled his face against any telegraphing expressions and opened the bet with a dollar. Schohn stroked his chin, called and raised another dollar. Hollendorfer chuckled and called the raise. Then, with a smug smile, he sweetened the pot another two dollars. Ferl, the ever cautious player, thought long and hard before he called the bet, figuring his pair of kings stood a good chance of picking up a partner on the draw.

Brad called, which decreased the stack of money before him. But he felt confident. Like an ocean wave that rolls powerfully back to shore, he again tasted the euphoria of the gambling fever and raised another dollar.

Ferl threw down his cards in disgust and Hollendorfer chuckled some more.

"You must have a crackerjack hand, boy," Hollendorfer commented.

Brad kept his face impassive. "It will cost you a dollar to find out."

"Well, I'm just so plum curious I'll just call that bet of yours."

Schohn contemplated the splay of cards in his fingers, holding them closer to his vest than Brad had remembered him doing in the previous hands. This hand had become serious business, and Schohn intended to win it. Hollendorfer just looked amused and that gave Brad a moment of concern. But his three aces looked good, and he still had the draw to come. He grinned back at the bearded man across the table from him while Schohn made up his mind.

Ferl was out of the game and now he leaned back in his chair with his cards face down on the table. He watched Brad make a careful study of his hand and whistled softly when Brad discarded only one card. "The boy is holding a genuine hand," he declared, passing a single card back to him.

Brad had discarded his four. His breath caught when he picked up the card dealt to him. Ferl had given him another king. A full house! The corners of his lips twitched and he struggled to keep a grin from showing.

Schohn asked for two cards. They seemed to make a difference and he let go of a breath that had been caught in his throat.

"I'll take two," Hollendorfer said and sorted them clumsily into his hand with that same amused smile on his face.

Brad concentrated on the three aces and two kings in his fingers. *Now there's a betting hand*, his Uncle Jethro would have said, and Brad wholeheartedly agreed.

"Ten dollars," Brad said carelessly, pushing the coins into the center of the table.

Ferl grinned and watched Schohn's face go through a parade of contortions. Schohn's eyes moved back and forth between Hollendorfer's unchanging smile and Brad's strained poker face. His own pile of coins had diminished considerably since Brad had joined the game and now the kid was going to take more away from him. Was he only bluffing? Schohn wondered as he glanced at Hollendorfer's face. But that told him nothing. Hollendorfer's grin wasn't unusual, he decided. Hollendorfer always grinned. Since his accident, Malcolm Hollendorfer had stopped taking life—and poker—very seriously. He had rubbed shoulders with the devil, as he had often said, and now just being among the living was joy enough for him.

Schohn's hands were sweating, but he wasn't going to allow the kid to bluff him out of the money he had already invested in the game. He held a pair of queens and a pair of jacks which he had just drawn. It seemed good enough to call the kid's bet.

Hollendorfer didn't hesitate. He called the bet then grinned at Brad and said, "All right, hotshot cardplayer. It cost me a dollar to stick last time around. I'm giving you the same choice. Only this will cost you a mite more. I see you got twenty-eight dollars left showing. I'm gonna play it square with you, kid. I'm only gonna raise you twenty-eight dollars."

The huge pile of money in the center of the table tripled by Hollendorfer's raise. More money than Brad had seen in his life, and a goodly portion of it his. He held a full house, aces and kings, a *betting hand!* And it was all going to be his! He couldn't lose! He knew he couldn't lose. Yet that act of pushing his final twenty-eight dollars into the pot brought on a lump of apprehension that caused him to swallow hard. But afterwards, with his money there with the rest of it, he felt confident and looked at a moist-browed Ernest Schohn and said, "Well, you in, mister?"

"Don't push me, kid," he said sharply.

Hollendorfer chuckled softly.

Schohn looked at Brad, looked at the empty table where Brad's money had been, then glanced at his own small pile of coins. He had a dollar less than thirty left and suddenly a thought occurred to him. A slow smile began to move across his lips. "Sure, I'm in, kid. Here's my twenty-eight dollars to call, and here's another dollar for my raise. See it or fold." Schohn didn't care that Hollendorfer could take it all now, using the same ploy. Malcolm Hollendorfer was the only one with money showing, but it wouldn't matter. It was the kid Schohn was after and he'd lose it all for the pleasure of seeing Brad go down with him.

Hollendorfer frowned. It wasn't the way he preferred to play cards, but Schohn was in his rights to raise. He called Schohn's raise. "Boy, I hope you got another dollar on you somewheres. If'n you don't, you'll have to fold."

"But I don't. That's all the money I got!"

"Too bad, kid," Schohn said, grinning.

Brad looked back at his hand, startled and confused. It was a *betting hand!* It would have taken the pot! He couldn't let it end this way.

Schohn was already directing his attention to Hollendorfer. "Looks like this is just between you and me now, Malcolm."

"I'm in," Hollendorfer said adding his dollar.

"Wait! I got this. It's worth a sight more than one dollar. It's real gold and listen—" Brad opened the lid and the watch began to play "Yankee Doodle."

"Let me see that, boy." Hollendorfer held the watch close to his good eye. "Ain't that pretty. You sure you want to bet it?"

"Yes."

"In that case I'd say it should cover, don't you, Ernest?" Schohn mumbled and nodded his head.

"What you got, boy?"

Brad laid down his full house. Schohn cussed and threw his cards on the table and headed for the bar.

"Ernest doesn't like to lose," Ferl commented dryly.

"I don't blame him." Brad reached for the pot.

Hollendorfer cleared his throat. "Hold up there, boy. I don't much care to lose either," he said, and he laid down five hearts.

Hollendorfer pocketed Brad's watch, after opening it to listen to the melody one more time. Brad didn't move. For a moment he thought it all a big joke and any time they'd break out laughing. But it wasn't a joke. No one was laughing. He'd lost, lost everything. He struggled not to show a tear and left the table in a daze.

EIGHT

LONG SHADOWS tugged the afternoon towards evening. Brad and Danny found a bench to sit on while they pondered the dilemma before them. With no money in their pockets, Danny was becoming uncomfortably aware of a grumbling within his stomach. A grumbling that in not too many more hours would be a downright emptiness. Already the dinner he'd enjoyed at The Old Homestead seemed a long way in the past. With empty pockets Danny could expect no more food until they reached Aunt Lucy's place in Trinidad, and that wouldn't be until late the following day. He scowled irritably at his older brother.

Brad had other concerns on his mind as he watched the shadows march steadily up the street. With no money he could forget the lovely Crystal Lane, but that loss now seemed inconsequential compared to the loss of his grandfather's gold watch. Somehow it must be recovered!

"I told you you ought to forget it!" Danny said suddenly.

Brad shot a glance at his little brother, but Danny had been right. They'd have been far better off going back to the depot to await the two-forty train. Far better still if they had stayed on their train in Colorado Springs. They would be in Trinidad by now, safe and drinking milk and eating oatmeal cookies in Aunt Lucy's kitchen. He'd still have his watch, too.

"We got to figure a way to get Grandpa's watch back."

Danny looked at him. "How you reckon we can do that? We ain't got no more money, and that one-eyed man sure ain't gonna give it back to you."

"I don't know. Maybe we can steal it from him."

"No!" Danny said. "No, we ain't gonna do that. We got in enough trouble today. Best we just forget it and leave it all behind when the train comes."

"But it was Grandpa's watch!"

"I know." Danny frowned and kicked his suitcase. "Shoot, Brad, why'd you ever go and bet it in the first place?"

"I had a winning hand."

"Well, it didn't win us nothing but hardship, Brad."

"All right, I messed up, I know. Don't kick a man when he's down."

"Come on, Brad, let's go back to the depot. I don't like being on the street when it gets dark."

"Grandpa's watch," Brad reminded him.

"It's gone."

"No! I'll get it back. I have to. Besides, what will we ever tell Ma and Pa? I can't tell them I lost it in a poker game. They can't never know we came to Cripple Creek instead of going straight to Trinidad."

"Yeah, that could get us both whipped. Hey, where you going?"

Brad had hoisted his grip and started back down towards Myers Avenue. "I don't know, but sitting here ain't going to get anything done."

"Psssst."

They stopped, startled.

"Hey, kids."

Brad looked around, saw the man standing in the recess of a doorway, back where the late afternoon light ended. "You talking to us, mister?"

The man beckoned to them. "Sure, kid, you don't see no one else about, do you? Come here."

Danny held back, giving Brad second thoughts.

"What do you want, mister?" Brad asked.

"Got a deal for you two."

"A deal?"

"Yeah, come a little closer."

"You come out here," Danny said.

"Naw, can't do that."

"Why not?" Danny inquired.

The man grinned around a cigar in his teeth. He wore a dark jacket and a round crown hat with a narrow brim. He was built like a beer barrel with legs, a good half a head shorter than Brad. He pointed a stubby forefinger at his eyes. "Can't come out where the light is bright. Had some dynamite go off whilst I was watching it. Nearly blinded me. Now bright lights make 'em burn like the devil's own flames."

"Gosh," Danny said.

Brad took his brother's hand and went up the steps into the doorway. "What kind of deal you got?"

"What's your name, boy?"

"Brad Medford."

"Medford? You new around here?"

"Just arrived."

"Good, that's good."

"Why?"

"My name is Tollar. Jake Tollar."

Brad shook hands. Tollar leaned back into the shadow of the doorway. "I couldn't help overhearing you two a moment ago. Sounds like a tight fix you got yourselves into, what with no money and all."

Brad didn't like the smile that seemed perpetually frozen on Tollar's face. "We're a little down on our luck, but we can manage."

The smile broadened. Tollar removed the cigar and said, "Good. You got spirit, boy. I like that. Maybe I can help out some. How much money you two need?"

Brad's mind was a sudden blank. How much would he need to buy back his gold watch?

"Ten dollars!" Danny said firmly. Tollar looked at him, then stuck the cigar back between his teeth.

"Ten dollars? That sounds like a reasonable sum."

"Apiece."

Tollar's glance narrowed. "Well now, I . . ."

"What we got to do?" Brad broke in. "We ain't doin' nothin' that ain't legal."

"Do I look like a man who'd break the law?" Tollar said with a look of indignation, letting the subject of money drop for the moment. "Why, my mother, bless her soul, would plum roll over in her grave if I didn't treat all men like my very own brother. No, sir, what I want to hire you two to do —at a reasonable price—" he added, with a glance at Danny, "is strictly honest work. Honest work, I repeat, and won't take but an hour of your time and won't hardly feel like work at all." He ended with his hand upon his chest and a look of deep sincerity upon his face.

"I don't know," Danny hesitated.

"Fifteen dollars—that's seven-fifty *apiece*."

"We'll do it!"

"But, Brad—"

"I know what I'm doing," Brad said sharply.

"He ain't even told us what we have to do yet, Brad."

"He said it was legal."

Tollar rubbed his palms together. "Good, good. My brother, Justin, is inside." He opened the door and waved an arm at the darkened interior.

Brad stepped through and immediately thought of The Old Homestead's parlor. Compared to this, it was a slice of sunshine. He entered the dark room and looked around at the sparse furnishings, drab and dusty behind the drawn curtains. Along one wall rose a staircase and the blackness at the top surpassed the gloominess of the parlor.

"Up there?" Brad asked with a gulp.

Tollar grinned around the cigar in his lips. "My brother will explain it all."

* * *

"I was keeping an eye on Kraker's office like you told me—"

Bernard Horschmann slammed his whiskey glass onto the table top and glared at the fat little man. "I didn't tell you to get caught!"

"I couldn't help it," Rawlin whined.

"What did you tell him?"

"Nothing, honest. I just told him I was minding my own business."

"Did he believe you?"

"I don't think so."

Horschmann cursed, lifted his glass and cursed again, discovering it was empty. He rapped it on the table, motioning for another bottle. "Who was this stranger?"

"I didn't ask his name. What with him holding the gun, he was asking most of the questions."

"You carry a gun?"

Boyd Rawlin dropped his eyes to his pudgy hands. "He took it away from me."

Horschmann gave a short, impatient laugh. "I wonder why I keep you around. I ask you to do a simple thing like keep an eye on Ben Kraker's office and you make a mess of it."

"I did learn that he's a marshal. That's something," Rawlin came back in his own defense.

"Yeah, that's something," Horschmann conceded. "That means they're getting ready to take Harry out. The question is, when?"

Karl Rheutters leaned across the table. "I can find out," he said in a low voice. "I'll send some of the boys to ask around."

Horschmann fingered an old scar under his chin. "Yeah, do that. Then come back here so we can make plans. If that marshal is taking Harry, he'll most likely be leaving in the morning. I want everything ready by then."

"Right." Rheutters left the table.

"What do you want me to do?"

Horschmann looked at him. "You best stay out of sight, but be handy in case I need you. Oh, and get yourself another gun."

"He said I can pick mine up from Kraker."

"You stay away from Kraker, hear?"

"Right. I . . . I'll just get a new one."

"You do that, Rawlin. And make sure you don't run into that marshal again. Now get out of here."

Boyd Rawlin hurried out the back door and Bernard Horschmann poured another drink from the bottle as it arrived at his table. He thought of Crystal Lane and then that boy. . . . He'd pass the word around that here was five dollars for the man who brought the kid to him. He tossed back the whiskey. It burned his throat and he grinned. He'd have her. One way or the other, he'd have her. And the kid would pay for butting his nose where it didn't belong.

Both were foregone realities in Horschmann's mind and he set them aside now, working out the plans for his brother's escape. It would have to go just right. The men had to be in place when Ben Kraker walked Harry down to the depot. It had to go like clockwork. Ambushing and killing two lawmen was not a thing to be taken lightly. He'd put a lot of thought into it and now he itched to put the daring scheme into action.

NINE

JUSTIN TOLLAR was a tall, willowy man with a Lincoln jaw that jutted forward and a shock, of wiry, black hair. He paced across the floor, turned and raised a finger as if to make a point to the other occupant of the room when the door opened and Brad and Danny stepped in.

"What the—?" He glanced at Jake. "Who are these boys?"

"They're lookin' for a job, Justin."

"A job?"

Jake moved close to Justin's ear. In a moment the Lincoln jaw tilted up and a thin smile moved across his face.

"So," Justin said, smiling down at the boys, "you two need a job, is it?"

"Yes, sir," Brad said, embarrassed at the timidity that showed in his voice.

"They need a job, Margaret," Justin said, turning to the woman who stood across the room in the pale light that filtered through a dingy window pane.

Her oval face turned from the window and the fading sunlight touched red hair, piled high, setting it aglow. Brad could not make out her features in the backlight of the window, but he received the impression of weariness. Not weariness that comes with hard work, but a more subtle kind. As if life itself had worn her down. She wore a blue pastel dress and her hands clutched a black book at her waist.

"So?" she commented with disinterest.

Justin Tollar went to her, put an arm over her shoulder

and bent close to her ear. When she turned back again, she studied Brad and Danny with new interest.

"The little one will do fine. I don't know about the tall one, though," she said.

"We can find something for him to do," Justin replied, stroking his long chin.

Jake Tollar said, "Maybe we can do like we did in Parkerville."

"Parkerville." Margaret laughed. "You mean disasterville."

"No, wait, Jake has a point." Justin paused to rearrange his thoughts, then looked back at Margaret, smiling. "Yes, I think that will work fine."

"I don't know, Justin."

"Sure. It will be fine. We can use . . . er, I mean, we can employ both these fine young lads . . . but first—" He stood over the boys and looked solemnly into their faces.

"First, what?" Brad asked, fidgeting.

Justin Tollar motioned to Margaret and she slapped the black book into his hand. He brought it before the boys and placed it firmly between both his palms. "But first, boys, I must know . . ." He paused.

Danny gulped when Justin's eyes widened and his voice began to tremble.

"Are you two Believers?"

"Believers?" Brad asked.

"In the Word! The Holy Word of God!"

"Yes . . . yes, sir." Brad faltered and Danny knew by the sudden fervor rising in Tollar's voice that any moment fire and brimstone would start raining down about them. "Ma used to take us to camp meetings."

"Praise the Lord!" Justin bellowed, raising his Bible towards the ceiling. "Then tonight you will help us do the Lord's work, right here in the sin-filled streets of Cripple Creek."

"Gosh," Brad said.

Startled, Danny glanced up into Justin Tollar's fevered eyes and, more than ever, wished they had stuck to their original course. Suddenly the safety and warmth of Aunt Lucy's kitchen seemed far away. At the moment he cared little for the promised seven dollars and fifty cents and would have traded it all for Aunt Lucy's warm lap, a plate of her oatmeal cookies and a glass of cold milk.

* * *

Walt Devon rolled heavily on the lower bunk and came suddenly awake, wary and alert. In a moment he relaxed and opened his eyes. The slanting light through the window reached to the back wall now. A uniformed police officer occupied one of the desks and Ben Kraker was hunched over another, digging through a stack of papers there. In the next cell, restless pacing drew his attention.

Harry Horschmann stopped his pacing and looked at Devon. "You snore, old man," he said.

Devon gave a short laugh and stood. "It means I'm still breathing, young fellow. At my age snoring is a reassuring sound."

Ben glanced up from his paperwork.

"Have a good nap, Walt?"

Devon took his gunbelt from the hook and strapped it around his wide waist. "It's a damned nuisance, Ben, having to grow old. But, considering the alternative, I reckon I can concede to a nap now and then."

Horschmann gripped the bars and sneered between them. "When my brother, Bernard, has his way with you, you won't need to worry about snoring anymore, old man."

Devon swung around and Horschmann backed away from the bars. Devon grinned at him, then looked back at Ben Kraker. "That boy has a mouth, don't he?"

"Yeah, and I've had to live with that mouth since I arrived."

"The boy won't be so chesty when I take him out tonight, Ben. Fact is, he'll probably wet his britches when the train rolls out and his big, bad brother hasn't sprung him."

Harry Horschmann swung back with the tin cup, then thought better of it and flung it to the floor. He kicked the cup into the corner and went back to pacing the cell.

Devon grinned. "What time you have, Ben?"

"Quarter to six."

"I'm going to take a walk. Maybe get a bite to eat."

Ben lowered his voice. "You mean you're going to check over the town before you take him out, don't you?"

Devon shrugged his shoulders. "When you expect trouble, it's best to know the lay of the land before it hits, don't you think?"

Kraker frowned. "You take care, Walt."

"I always do."

Devon started for the door, then paused and looked back at Kraker. "That fellow ever come for his gun, Ben?"

"Nope." Kraker leaned back in the chair. "Been unusually quiet day—except for one of the local call girls who had a bad experience with some rotten apples." He refrained from naming Bernard Horschmann in front of Harry.

"She get hurt?"

"Nope. She was lucky. Two boys showed up in time and broke it up."

Devon looked up sharply, aware of a sudden uneasiness. He'd had the same feeling earlier and had shrugged it off. He wasn't prepared to shrug it off a second time. "Two boys?" he asked.

"Yeah, brothers they were. I think they were out to see if the stories they heard of Cripple Creek were true. I sure hope they get back to their train before they get themselves into trouble. They're too green for the likes of Myers Avenue."

"Did you get their names, Ben?"

"The ones who attacked the girl?"

"The boys."

Ben Kraker stroked his chin. "Well, I don't know now . . . yeah, I seem to recall the one. It was Brad something. Mumfort or Memfort—"

"Medford?"

"Yeah, that was it, Walt. Brad Medford. I didn't get the younger one's name." Kraker looked confused. "How'd you know?"

"I rode up with them on the train."

"Well, they shouldn't be wandering around town like they are with no one to watch over them. Too bad, them being orphans and all."

"Orphans? Is that what they told you?"

"That's what he told me." Kraker's eyes narrowed. "Those boys lie to me, Walt?"

Devon laughed. "They're no more orphans than I am President McKinley. They're covering their hind ends, that's what they're doing, Ben. That older one, Brad, has got a bee in his bonnet about the girls along Myers Avenue. He figures he's got some serious growing up to do and he wants to get it done without word reaching back to his folks. Orphans!"

Kraker shook his head and grinned. "Sounds like something we'd have done in our younger days, Walt."

"I figure us for having more sense than that, Ben."

"Not if I remember straight."

Devon tugged his hat down on his head and smiled reminiscently. "I reckon you might be right about that, Ben. Talk to you later."

The evening was pleasant and the traffic on the sidewalks had thinned. Along the street tall brick buildings touched the darkening sky. They were mostly flat-roofed and come nightfall a man up there with a rifle would be impossible to see. There were also the windows facing the street that presented danger. Devon turned the corner and strolled down to the next street. He paused at the corner and studied Myers Avenue. It was no better than Bennett Avenue for his purposes. Tall brick buildings, dark windows . . . but here there seemed to be more night life. An electric trolley rattled up the street on narrow tracks, its bell clanging as it turned a corner.

Devon shook his head in amazement. He continued along Myers Avenue a way, turned into a saloon and made his way through the smoky room to the bar.

"What'll it be, mister?" a fellow in a smudged apron asked.

"Whiskey," he said, turning to study the barroom and the clutter of miners that filled the tables and hung along the bar.

The whiskey came. Devon paid the man and took a sip. A sound from the far end of the saloon drew his attention. He levered himself off the bar, taking the drink with him, and shouldered through a knot of men standing around a table.

Malcolm Hollendorfer snapped the watch lid closed and popped it open again to the delight of the miners, who became suddenly silent as the little watch played "Yankee Doodle."

"That's a fancy watch, mister," Devon said.

Hollendorfer glanced up and narrowed his one eye against the ceiling lamp that showed over Devon's left shoulder. This stranger was certainly not a miner, Hollendorfer knew. Too old, for one thing. The heavy revolver at Devon's hip also bespoke of a different trade than swinging a pick. He noticed the glint of polished nickel pinned to Devon's chest, partly hidden by the dark wool vest. "It sure is, ain't it?"

"Not many like it around, I suspect."

Hollendorfer scratched an itch under his eye patch. "I suspect not."

Devon shifted his weight in the tight quarters and rested his right hand upon the ivory-gripped pistol. A purely natural move, a comfortable stance, which over the years he'd learned to take without much thought. Now it amused him as the miners gave ground to it. "I've only seen one other like it. It was owned by a young boy about seventeen."

Hollendorfer grinned. "I come by this watch honestly, sheriff."

"Marshal."

"All right. I won it off the boy you're talking about in a card game, fair and square . . . marshal."

Devon smiled at him. He tapped the shoulder of the fellow occupying the nearest chair, hooked a finger under his suspender strap and eased him out of the seat. The man came out of it without argument, seemed instead anxious to be somewhere else. Devon swung a leg over the back of the vacated chair and settled down across from Hollendorfer. He signaled the barkeep. "A whiskey here for my friend."

An uneasy smile inched across Hollendorfer's face. When the drink arrived, Devon said, "Suppose you tell me all about this card game."

"Why? You his old man?"

A twinge of guilt shot through Devon as he thought of Ferro, then he put his son out of mind. "Let's just say I'm an interested party."

Hollendorfer shrugged his shoulders. "Sure." He raised the glass to his lips and poured half down his throat. "I'll tell you what you want to know, marshal." He glanced at the glass in his hand. "I reckon you paid to hear it."

When he had finished with the story of the card game and his winning the watch, Hollendorfer leaned back in his chair and watched Devon silently contemplate his own empty glass.

Finally Devon said, "What happened to the boy afterward?"

"I don't know, marshal. He left with another boy, younger than himself, who was waiting for him outside. I never did get a good look at him."

"He didn't say where he was going?"

"Nope. I suspect there wasn't anyplace for him to go but home, seeing as he was flat broke after losing the watch."

"Maybe back to the depot," Devon said to himself aloud.

"Maybe," Hollendorfer commented.

Devon frowned and kicked back his chair, standing. "Well, I suppose I better go find him before he gets himself into more trouble. Thanks for the information."

"Any time, marshal."

Devon started to leave then swung back and studied Hollendorfer's face a moment. "You wouldn't consider selling that watch to me?"

"Well, now, I don't know, marshal. A man don't often

come by **such a fine** watch as this." He paused and stroked his chin **contemplatively.** "I suppose if I did sell it, it wouldn't **be cheap."**

Devon **figured as** much.

TEN

BOTH SIDES of Myers Avenue presented the same problem. Any alleyway, any darkened window, any rooftop could conceal an ambush. He stopped when he reached the cribs tucked under the trestle at Poverty Gulch at the end of Myers. The shacks shook with activity and drunken laughter came from the curtained windows. The wind shifted. Devon recoiled at the stench and turned back, veering up the steep incline of Second Street towards Bennett Avenue.

At Bennett he paused a moment to catch his breath; the thin mountain air sapped his strength. Not one to allow the altitude to defeat him, Devon continued on towards the depot. The character of Cripple Creek changed here; the businesses were of a respectable nature, as if all the saloons and whorehouses and gambling houses and opium dens were the private domain of Myers Avenue. That wasn't true, he knew, but at least Bennett Avenue presented a respectable side, whereas respectability was nowhere to be found one street below.

Devon pushed those thoughts from his mind and pondered the problem of transporting his prisoner. Ahead the brick, three-story Midland Terminal Railroad building loomed in the dying light of evening and Bennett Avenue ended at its front steps. There was really no good way to walk Harry Horschmann up to it without exposing himself and Ben to a dozen different possible directions of attack. *Well, when you can't go around a bear, you go through him and, when the fur settles, hope you're still standing.* He shrugged his shoulders and went up the steps.

The six-thirty train for Colorado Springs was being boarded, and Devon didn't see Brad or Danny among those clutching grips and standing in line. He checked the coaches and returned through the terminal. Outside, he paused on the front step and a movement of people pulled his eyes towards a large canvas tent erected on a vacant lot to his right. Above the opened door-flap were painted the words: *Jesus Heals*. He recalled a poster he'd seen advertising a Reverend Justin Tollar and a tent meeting he was conducting at seven.

On a hunch he started towards the tent, then wheeled to a stop. Considering what Brad had come to Cripple Creek for, Devon figured a tent meeting would be the last place he'd find the boys. He walked back into town, to the Merchant's Cafe, and took the same table he'd occupied for lunch.

The place was nearly empty. The tall, long-faced girl who came through a back door had large brown eyes that seemed to disappear in their fleshy sockets and red hair tied up in a bun. Her skin was pallid, but the creases along her cheek bespoke of another time where wind and sun had been harsh and shelter scarce. Now, however, she spent much time indoors and only an outbreak of freckles across her nose colored her otherwise drawn face. When she saw Devon, a smile brightened her tired face. She wiped her hands on the apron around her waist and came to his table.

"Evening, sir." Her voice was pleasant, with more life to it than Devon had expected. "What can I get you?"

"Whatever is on the back stove will be fine, and some coffee and a slice of apple pie if you have it."

"Peach cobbler is the best I can do," she said. "The mister just finished turning some ice cream; the two together would make a pleasant finish to the stew we have on the stove."

"The cobbler sounds just fine."

"Dark bread or light?"

"Dark."

"Be right out with your coffee." She looked at him closer. "You're a peace officer, aren't you?"

"Yes, ma'am."

"How interesting." Her face showed some previously hidden life. "I haven't seen you before. New in town?"

"Just arrived."

"Staying long?"

"No. Soon as I take care of business, I'll be leaving."

"Seeing as you're a peace officer," she smiled, "I think I can talk the mister into giving you cobbler and coffee on the house. How does that sound?"

Devon grinned. "Sounds real nice. Now I know why Ben Kraker recommended this place."

"You a friend of Ben?"

Devon nodded his head. "Ben and I go back a lot of years, more than I care to recollect sometimes."

"Ben is a nice man. He only recently arrived too, you know."

"So he tells me."

She broadened her smile. "I'll get your coffee, Mr.—" She paused.

"It's Devon, ma'am. Walter Devon."

"Mr. Devon." She hurried away, Devon couldn't help but notice, with a livelier step than she'd had only a few moments ago. He discovered he was smiling.

The clock on the wall struck the hour. Seven o'clock. Eight hours until his train was to leave. So far the only threat to him taking his prisoner down to the depot for the early morning train was Ben Kraker's own fear of what Harry's brother, Bernard, might do to break him out. And those fears came from Bernard Horschmann's reputation, not from a direct threat. Bernard had kept a low profile and, according to Ben, that was not Horschmann's usual way— another link in the chain of suspicion Ben had forged for himself and in turn draped over Devon's shoulders.

With these suspicions, real or not, it would be foolish not to work out some plan to take Harry Horschmann out, even if it were only to enlist the help of the half-dozen constables at Kraker's disposal. Eight armed men marching down to the depot instead of two would be a stronger deterrent if Bernard Horschmann were planning to free his brother.

He had not come to Cripple Creek expecting trouble. He'd done this sort of work often enough to think of it as another routine job. Now he had some rethinking to do.

Their position was not a defensible one. The dark alleys, windows and rooftops were made to order for an ambush, which Devon felt would be the probable avenue of attack on them. The modern jail was too well-constructed and the depot would be too crowded and besides both of those places offered cover. The open street between was a long dangerous walk and that's where they would strike.

"You look puzzled, marshal."

He had not heard her come up. He erased the scowl and replaced it with a smile. "Just thinking," he told her.

"Then it must be serious thoughts." She placed his coffee on the table. "I can have dinner out now, or would you prefer to have some time with your coffee first?"

"I'm in no great hurry. I have lots of time on my hands. What's your name?"

"Didi, Didi Ross." Her lips wrinkled together in a funny smile. "Actually, my real name is Deirdre." Color came to her cheeks. "But that's too fancy a name for someone like me."

"It's a pretty name. Deirdre . . . that's Irish, isn't it?"

"Yes, it is."

Devon glanced around the cafe. "Business is slow."

"Usually is this time of the evening. We will be closing up shortly."

"Have you lived in Cripple Creek long, Deirdre?"

She laughed. "No one has lived in Cripple Creek very long, marshal. Eight years ago there was nothing here but a cow camp and a fellow named Bob Womack. Then he discovered gold in what is now Poverty Gulch and, poof, overnight there was Cripple Creek, born a full-grown city."

"How long have you been here?"

Deirdre sighed and sat down in a chair across the table. "Too long, Mr. Devon. I came five years ago. Worked here and there to keep body and soul together; then I met the mister." She nodded her head at the door to the kitchen. "We married and opened this cafe."

"Where is home?" Devon sipped the coffee

A smile crept across her face, then fled. "My folks have a cow camp out east. I grew up punching cows and shoeing horses . . . among other things. When I got old enough, I wanted to see what a real city was like. So I came to Cripple Creek."

"Miss it?"

"Sometimes," she sighed. "It was hard work, punching cows, but at least at night, when you went to bed, it was so quiet and peaceful. That's one thing about a city, marshal, the town never sleeps. There is never any real peace and quiet."

"I know what you're saying."

"How about you, marshal. What kind of business brings you to Cripple Creek?"

"State business. I've come to pick up a prisoner. To take him down to the penitentiary."

"Oh, so you're the one come for Bernard's brother."

"That's right."

"Everyone heard about what Harry did. The trial was big news. Then, of course, I know Ben Kraker. He comes in every now and again. He told me the prison was sending someone to pick Harry up."

"What do you know about the brother, Bernard?" Devon asked her.

Deirdre's face wrinkled into a frown. "He's not a nice man, from what I hear. He has the town under his thumb. Not the whole town, mind you, just that segment that hasn't the right connections or the political strong arms to protect themselves. He leaves the mines strictly alone. They'd crush him in a minute. And he stays clear of the miners, too. The Western Federation of Miners is a lot stronger than he is and he knows it. Bernard Horschmann is shrewd when it comes to his business dealings."

Devon detected the bitterness in her voice. "Then who does he hurt?" he asked.

Deirdre shrugged a narrow shoulder. "The smaller businesses. The people who can't afford to buy protection and can't afford to lose what they have if they don't play along with Horschmann."

"People like you and your husband."

She glanced down at her hands and nervously wiped them on her apron. "We make out all right," she said, standing. "I'll go get your dinner now, marshal. Here I am taking up all your time and you must be hungry. Besides, I shouldn't be sitting around talking when I have my work to do."

The stew and bread arrived along with a bowl of butter. Deirdre refilled Devon's coffee cup, then vanished behind the closed kitchen door. She reappeared off and on to greet customers and collect from those leaving.

When Devon finished his meal, she brought out warm cobbler topped with vanilla ice cream but, instead of hurrying off again, paused at the table and wiped her hands on the apron.

"Marshal—" Her hands wrung the apron tighter. "Are you planning to leave soon?"

He looked at her, unsure of the meaning of her question. Deirdre cleared her throat and said, "I mean Cripple Creek, not the cafe. When do you plan to take Harry Horschmann out of town? Tomorrow?"

"In a few hours," Devon replied, glancing at the clock.

"You mean tonight, then?"

"The train leaves at two-forty."

Deirdre masked her tension with a quick smile. "I . . . I just wanted to tell you to be careful. I mean, well, Bernard Horschmann is not one to let kinfolk go without a fight."

"So I've been told."

She smiled, the tension drained from her fingers, a blush came to her pale cheeks. "Well, that's all I wanted to say. Just be careful, that's all." She turned away abruptly and hurried back to the kitchen, glancing briefly over her shoulder as she pushed through the door. The spring hinges closed it behind her.

Devon watched the door flop back and settle in place. He frowned. Another warning. Perhaps it was time to take them more seriously. He fingered the spoon again and dug into the steaming cobbler.

ELEVEN

MARGARET MERCIE tugged Brad's head around.

"Ouch!" he howled rubbing his ear.

"Pay attention to what I'm telling you, boy."

"You leave my brother alone!" Danny bunched his shoulders.

"And you hush up."

"I will not!"

"Then leave right this minute and forget about getting paid."

Brad put a hand on Danny's shoulder. "It's all right, Danny." He needed that money desperately and, if going through with this would get it for him, well then, he'd do it.

Danny eased back and from inside the big tent Justin Tollar's dynamic voice rose up a fevered scale. Danny glanced at the illuminated sheets of canvas.

"And Jesus said in Matthew 17:20, if ye have faith as a grain of mustard seed, ye shall say unto this mountain, remove hence to yonder place; and it shall be removed; and nothing shall be impossible unto you. . . . My dear people do you believe this?"

Justin paused and the silence flowed back.

"I say, do you believe this? Say 'Amen'!"

"Amen," came a tentative response.

"I want to hear Amen!" Justin bellowed.

"Amen!" the crowd came back.

Margaret pushed a crutch into Brad's hand. "Let me see you use it."

He hobbled around in the darkness behind the tent, with

Justin Tollar's angular form, larger than life, silhouetted against the canvas wall and Justin's fiery words stabbing out at him with suffocating conviction.

"No, no, that's all wrong. Remember, you've been a cripple since birth. You have to appear as if you've been walking on a crutch all your life. Now, swing it out, but don't take too long a stride. And make it look like each step causes you pain."

Brad tried it again.

"That's better," Margaret said, standing back and studying his movements. "The crutch should be an extension of your arm. Grip it easier, not like you're hanging onto a bucking horse."

Brad hobbled around some more, then stopped and peered across the empty blackness behind the tent at Margaret. "I thought this was honest work. Seems to me deceiving all those people ain't quite honest—and Mr. Tollar being a preacher and all."

"That ain't none of your concern," Margaret began, but Jake Tollar intervened, smiling disarmingly.

"We aren't being dishonest, boys, even though it may appear as such," he said smoothly.

"What would you call it?" Danny asked.

"I'd call it lending help to those poor souls that need it most."

"You would?" Danny's voice rose in surprise.

"How do you figure?" Brad asked.

"You believe there is healing in the Word, don't you?"

Danny and Brad glanced at each other, then nodded their heads.

"Well, so does Reverend Tollar. He believes it so fervently that it just sets his soul on fire. His only desire in life is to be a channel for that healing power. Understand?"

"No," the boys said together.

Jake smiled. "Well, you see, the only way folks can receive healing is if they truly believe it's possible to be healed. Most folks are skeptical when it comes to healing. That's how we —you and I and Margaret—help those poor, sick people.

We show them a miracle. We show them the healing power of the Word. We show them that the lame *can* walk again, that the blind *can* see again . . . and they believe! Then they come forward in faith and receive true healing at the hands of Justin Tollar. Now do you understand?"

"No," Danny said.

"Well, you will. Wait and see." Jake Tollar took Danny by the shoulder and walked him to the mouth of the tent. Inside, rows of rough-hewed benches were crowded with people. At the far end of the tent upon a raised platform stood Justin Tollar, one arm at the moment stretched upward, the other extended with an open Bible upon his palm.

Danny couldn't quite catch all that Justin Tollar was carrying on about, but by the looks of terror mixed with astonishment on the faces of those people inside the tent, he decided Justin was preaching on hell fire, and he didn't really want to go inside. Jake nudged him on.

"Take my hand, boy, and no looking about."

"But I—" Danny protested, holding back.

Jake squeezed Danny's hand. "Don't you go giving me grief, boy, or you will be in sore need of healing for certain."

"Yes, sir." He winced, unable to wring his hand from Jake's grip.

"Good." Jake let up. "Remember what Margaret told you. Look straight ahead. You're not to take notice of anything around you and, when I take you up to Justin, I want you to stumble up the first step of the platform."

Danny nodded his head. They went into the tent, where the packed-in people and the smoky lanterns suspended from the center post made the air heavy with heat. Danny allowed himself to be guided, as they had instructed him, into an aisle where Jake found room enough to squeeze them in. He sat on the splintered wood and closed his eyes, trying not to think of what was to follow.

Brad stood outside the door, alone. A desperate urge to turn and flee welled up within him, but Danny was already inside. He couldn't turn tail and run, not now. He gulped down his misgivings and hobbled inside. A woman moved over to give him a place to sit, viewing the crutch first and then the boy, with pity in her eyes.

"Thank you, ma'am," he said, sliding in beside her. He wiped the sweat from his forehead and gripped the crutch with white knuckles. He glanced at Danny across the center aisle and quickly looked away, viewing instead the packed dirt at his feet. At least in the dirt he found no guilt.

* * *

"Hey . . . hey, Kraker. I need to use the privy."

Ben Kraker glanced up from the pile of papers that, of late, seemed to be the one overwhelming constant in his life. "Big city politics," he grumbled, tossing an impatient look at the faintly red-haired man leaning into the cell bars. They were alone at the moment and Ben wished there had been at least one of his constables there to whom he could delegate the chore. But there wasn't.

"Can't you hold it?"

"No, I can't and you won't want to clean it up neither."

"That's for damn certain," Kraker said under his breath. He removed a pair of shackles from a wall hook and tossed them to Harry. "Put 'em on."

Harry Horschmann snapped them around his ankles and stood back from the door, waiting for Kraker to insert the key, swing it open and unholster the pistol. He knew the routine. Down the back hallway Ben waited outside the privy door, heard the swish of the new water-flush system and stood back as Horschmann reappeared buttoning up his fly.

"Feel better?" Kraker commented dryly.

"Like a new man." Horschmann grinned disarmingly and then threw himself at the gun in Kraker's hand.

It caught Kraker off guard, and he cursed himself, realizing too late what had happened. The monotony of heavy loads of paperwork and working late into the night had lolled him into a state of dreamy complacency. He'd lost his edge and that was all it took for Horschmann to make his move.

Harry grabbed the gun and buried a shoulder in Kraker's

chest. They tumbled to the floor. Kraker struggled to keep the gun, but Horschmann was younger, stronger and desperate.

Harry kicked, but to no advantage with the shackles binding him. He swung a fist, missed and for an instant put himself at an angle that left him vulnerable. Ben seized the moment, released the gun and rammed an elbow into Harry's nose. Harry's hand left the pistol and Ben shoved it across the floor out of reach. He struggled to his feet, but Harry went for Ben's legs, knocking him back against the wall. Ben brought the heel of his boot down on Horschmann's wrist. Harry cried out and hugged the damaged hand to himself.

Ben staggered out of the hallway breathing heavily. He glanced at Harry and at the blood on the floor from Harry's broken nose. He wheeled around to recover his gun.

"Get up!" Ben gasped. "Get up or I'll plug you where you lay for attempting escape."

The urgency in Ben's voice sent a chilled shiver through Horschmann. The threat was genuine. Harry stared at the old man, now leaning against the wall for support and breathing heavily. "All right . . . all right, don't shoot," he said desperately. Blood flowed into his mouth and he sleeved it away with his left hand, favoring the right hand against his chest. He rose and scrambled into the cell. Kraker locked the door behind him and fell breathlessly into his chair.

"I need a towel," Horschmann complained. "I'm bleeding all over your damned jail cell, Kraker."

"Shut up." Kraker had to relax. He feared what was to come. He breathed deeply and tried to head it off, but then deep within his chest he felt the pangs radiating out: sharp, squeezing pains that worked their way into his arms and neck. Breathing became difficult. He clutched himself and dropped his head to the cluttered desk.

"Count," he told himself, remembering the doctor's instructions. "Slowly . . . one, breath, exhale . . . two, breath, exhale . . . three, breath, exhale . . ."

In five minutes the pain decreased and breathing became

easier. He lifted his head from the desk and looked wearily around, sleeving sweat from his brow.

"Hey, you all right, old man?"

Kraker craned his neck and seemed to recall that Harry had been speaking to him all along, but he couldn't remember what he had been saying. Horschmann's nose had quit bleeding. Drying blood smeared his cheeks and was beginning to crust along his upper lip.

"What's wrong, old man?" There was an unnatural concern in Harry's eyes. It rang in his voice.

Ben pushed himself to his feet, the floor lurched beneath his boots.

"You sick?"

He drew a basin of water and found a towel and handed them through the bars, then walked unsteadily out the front door into the cool evening air and sat upon a bench there, leaning his head back against the brick wall, closing his eyes.

"Damn close," he spoke softly to himself. Thank God he had remembered what that doctor in Denver had told him to do. Thank God he had had the time to do it. What was it the doctor had called it? He couldn't remember the fancy medical name, but it all boiled down to the same thing: his heart was going sour on him. If he wanted to see many more years, he'd have to stop working.

"Put me out to pasture," he mumbled suddenly, opening his eyes. The passerby merely nodded politely and continued on his way. "Put me out to pasture, like hell," Ben scoffed, closing his eyes again.

The pain drained away, as it always did, and he relaxed. He would like to go to sleep, but there was still the paperwork. And there was Devon, too. Walt would be taking his prisoner out in the morning; there'd be no sleeping tonight. Tomorrow he'd sleep late and maybe take the morning off. Do a little fishing perhaps. That was his usual promise to himself, he thought skeptically, as he rose wearily and went back inside.

Harry Horschmann, his face washed, his nose swollen,

watched Ben come in. "What's wrong with you, old man?" he demanded.

"Bear-wrestling damn fool young men like you," Ben replied, settling into his chair and shuffling the papers back into some semblance of order.

TWELVE

DEIRDRE ROSS stole a glance back over her shoulder at Devon as she pushed through the kitchen door. Inside the hot kitchen she let go of a breath that had buried itself deep within her. The flapping door settled back into place.

"Well?" Charlie Ross said over the bubbling black pot of stew, into which he was pouring water to thin the final few servings that remained.

She leaned against the door frame, staring at the tile floor beneath her feet.

"Charlie, I don't like this."

"It ain't your place nor mine to like."

"But he's such a nice old man," she replied, peeking out at Devon through a small, diamond-shaped window in the door.

"So? We're nice people, too, ain't we? Ain't no reason why we should bring pain on ourselves."

"Oh, how I hate that man!" Deirdre exploded suddenly, stomping a foot.

"Hush up, woman!" Charlie glanced apprehensively at the door that opened onto the back alleyway. "Don't you appreciate what you've got here?" His voice was an urgent whisper. "You want it all taken away, or worse yet, end up in a heap of ashes, like old man Robson's newspaper done last year?"

"No," Deirdre replied. She didn't know what she wanted.

"What did he say, Didi?"

She looked at her husband's round, sweaty face. He'd gained weight after he quit the mines to open their cafe three years ago. Gained it in his face, his arms and hands and the waist. But Didi didn't mind. She loved him. And Charlie Ross didn't seem to notice the imperfections in her either. They had built a comfortable life for themselves here, and if maintaining that comfort meant bending to the wills of the powers-that-be, well, there was always consolation in the dream that someday they'd have enough money to move out and live easier somewhere else.

Charlie had a way of justifying what had to be done to keep "moving ahead," as he put it. Didi didn't always see the logic of his reasoning, but she trusted him. He'd been born and bred in mining camps across the West, while she had known only the simple life of a cow camp and a family that loved and protected her. Didi's rationalization was to trust her husband's judgment, even if she didn't like it.

"He told me he was taking Harry down to the depot for the early train, the two-forty, I think he said."

Charlie set the pitcher down on the counter top and went to Deirdre. He took her shoulders in his large hands and kissed her forehead. Deirdre reached round him and laid her head upon his chest. Charlie was not a man who often allowed tenderness to display itself in any of his actions. When they were first married, Deirdre wondered if it was because of her that Charlie was reserved. Her plain features would make any man cold, she believed. But Charlie saw none of that. She knew it now. It was just his way and she treasured these few moments when he dropped his guard.

"Believe me, it's for the best," he said.

"Why does it have to be so?"

Charlie shrugged his shoulders. "Why does anything have to be so? It's life. It's our life here and if we want to stay we have to be careful."

"I'll say it again," she whispered softly against his chest, "I hate that man."

He looked grim and separated himself from her arms. "Go on, tell him and get it over with." Charlie went back to the pot of boiling stew. "Go on." He nodded at the back door. Deirdre went to it, her hand hesitated on the brass door knob a moment, then she pulled the door open.

In the dark alleyway the cherry glow of a cigar brightened. Karl Rheutters pushed off the brick wall and peered at Deirdre—a homely, horse-faced woman. He grinned. He recalled Crystal Lane and blood rushed into his brain. His eyes moved off Deirdre's face and carefully assessed the rest of her. Her body was strong and lithe and well-proportioned and Rheutters thought if he tried real hard he could imagine Crystal's face on Deirdre's shoulders. . . . Perhaps she was worth a try? After all, a woman with Didi's face should be starved for manly attention.

Deirdre flushed under Rheutters's open assessment and instinctively folded her arms about her waist. "I talked to him like you wanted."

Her words pulled him from his thoughts and brought him around again to the business at hand. He sucked the cigar; the tip lent a satanic glow to his face and arched eyebrows. "And?"

"And he is here to take Harry to the prison."

"When?"

"Tomorrow morning, early. The two-forty train."

"Two-forty A.M.?"

"Yes."

Rheutters looked concerned. "He wasn't planning it for that early," he said to himself.

"Planning what?" Deirdre asked.

Rheutters glanced up sharply. "Nothing. Forget it," he said and started away. He stopped and looked back at her.

In the darkness Didi thought he grinned. "Maybe later I'll come back, huh?" he said.

Deirdre shivered in the evening breeze. She turned away abruptly and went back inside, throwing the bolt as she closed the door.

Rhuetters's grin broadened. Maybe not, he told himself. Even with an imagined face she'd still look like a horse when it was over.

In the kitchen Deirdre stood gripping the door knob. Her

husband's reassuring voice gave her strength and she let go of it and squared her shoulders.

"You tell him?"

Deirdre nodded and pushed her fingers through her hair. "I told him."

"Good. Then let's forget it."

"That won't be easy," she replied evenly and moved to the kitchen door and peered through the small window. "He's ready to leave," she said. She found a smile somewhere within her, fixed it to her face and went out to the cash register.

"How was the dinner, marshal?"

"Like home cooking, ma'am. My compliments to the chef."

"I'll tell the mister. He'll be pleased. Dessert is on the house." She tried to look happy.

He smiled at Deirdre. "Thank you."

She watched him step out onto the sidewalk and return his hat to his head. He started down the street, stopped abruptly, changed his mind and moved off in the opposite direction. Then he was gone, leaving Deirdre with a heavy heart as she peered vacantly at the building across the street. It was the Weinberg Building, but she didn't really see it, nor was she thinking about such things.

* * *

Karl Rheutters bought a beer at the bar and carried it to the table in the corner. "I got some news I think you'll want to hear." He slid into a chair.

Bernard Horschmann looked up from his whiskey glass with blood-suffused eyes and a hand that trembled as it pressed against the tabletop to push him up straight in the chair.

Rheutters frowned. "You better lay off that stuff. We have a busy night ahead of us."

"What do you mean?"

"I mean that I found out about that marshal who's taking your brother to prison."

Horschmann's eyes narrowed soberingly. "What?"

"He's planning to take Harry out tonight."

"Tonight?"

"That's what the girl at the Merchant's Cafe said. He was eating his dinner there. I sort of suggested that if she didn't find out for us there might be an accidental fire or something at her business."

Horschmann grinned. "Good, that's the way to handle it. You catch on quick. That was always Harry's problem. He never caught on. That's why we had to leave Pennsylvania, why he's behind bars now." His grin broadened. "But I see big possibilities for you, Rheutters; you got proper attitude. Attitude, that's important."

Rheutters leaned back and sipped his beer contentedly. "That's true, but he's your brother just the same. What are you gonna do?"

Horschmann threw back the whiskey and set an empty glass on the table. "I got a plan, but I didn't expect him to be leaving tonight . . . what time?"

"Two-forty train to Colorado Springs."

"Two-forty." He tugged at his chin. "Yeah, that will work out even better. We'll have the darkness on our side."

"So will he," Rheutters reminded him.

"But he won't be expecting nothing. I made certain to stay clear of Harry. That new chief of police doesn't expect a thing, and neither does that marshal."

"I wouldn't count on it."

Horschmann thought a moment. "Maybe not." He rolled the empty glass between his palms. "Tell you what, you go out and round up Miller Thompson, Stu Gardner and Kenny Roberts. Tell them plans have changed and that I need them now."

"Anything else?"

"Yeah, on your way back stop off at my place and get my rifle." He pushed a key across the table. "Oh, and make sure you lock the door when you leave. This town is full of thieving bastards."

* * *

Afterward there **was always** the lingering pain, the dull, persistent ache in **the middle** of his chest—as if someone had dropped a rock there and just left it—that made itself known with each breath. The doc had told him it was worse with some people, while others hardly noticed it. Past experience told Ben it'd be several hours before he'd feel himself again. Each time it took a little longer to recover, but the worst was over and he could live with the minor annoyances. He had too much work to do to worry over it now. Still, he was worn out and he longed for the feather bed in his suite of rooms one story above.

He pushed aside the pile of posters he'd received that day and looked at the packet of signed transport papers on the corner of the desk. *Damn paperwork.* It wasn't like this in the old days. More and more he missed those earlier times. *Progress!*

The steady click, click, clicking came to a halt behind him. When he turned, Milo Johnson was watching him, his fingers poised in midair.

"Anything wrong, constable?" Ben seldom addressed his men that way.

"No, sir."

"Good. I thought perhaps that newfangled machine of yours broke down."

"No . . . I . . ." Milo looked back at the paper in front of him. He had noticed Ben's haggard, white face when he'd come in, noticed Ben's stiff, labored breathing. But he knew better than to fuss over the old man. Thank goodness he was talking of retirement now. Ben was a fine man to work under, but there finally comes a time for all men to ease back. "I was just thinking about what to put down next," Milo lied.

Kraker closed his eyes and the typewriter resumed its rhythmic clicking. In the background he listened to a muffled rattle and a clicking of another sort, not nearly as rhythmic as Johnson's typewriter. He is playing it cool, Kraker thought. Did he know for certain that his brother was going to spring him tonight? Kraker inhaled, felt his chest muscles tighten, smelled the pungent odor of pine from the newly milled wooden floors. Something told him to open his eyes. Devon was looking down at him.

"Didn't hear you come in, Walt," he said, straightening in his chair.

"When was the last time you had any sleep, Ben?"

Kraker shrugged his shoulders. "I'm all right."

"You look all done in."

"I said I'm fine." Kraker eased back and smiled. "Soon as tonight is over I'm gonna sleep fifteen hours straight, then go fishing. But thanks for being concerned, Walt."

Devon glanced at the cell. Harry Horschmann was sitting on the floor, his back to them, waving a fist in the air. He swung his fist and dice clattered along the floor, coming together in the corner of the cell.

"What's on your mind, Walt?" Kraker took the packet of signed transport papers in hand.

"I've had some time to think about him." Devon jabbed a thumb over his shoulder. Harry had gathered up the dice and was shaking them together in his fist again. "It might not be a bad idea to have a couple of your men on hand when we take him out tonight."

In the background the typewriter grew silent again.

Kraker pursed his lips, then wagged his white-haired head in agreement. "That same idea has crossed my mind too."

"How many men do you have?"

"Available? Not many."

"How many?"

"I'm supposed to have six full-time, but Mark Linely's boy has the measles. The whole house is in quarantine. Able Loss is out of town. That leaves four. But I can't guarantee I can round 'em all up on this short a notice. Johnson can round up those in town, but I'll have to send a rider out for Lew Mattsen. He lives on his brother's ranch about five miles from Cripple Creek.

"Three men, then."

Kraker nodded his head. "Think we'll need more?"

"I hope we don't need any at all."

"I'll get them." Kraker sent Milo Johnson out to fetch the other constables. Johnson seemed anxious to be free of the chore of typing up the day's report. Kraker motioned Devon to a chair. "Take the load off." He handed him the packet of papers. "There it is. All the damn paperwork. You'd think we was fixing to transport the crown jewels or something. I'll tell you, Walt, it ain't like the old days."

Devon patted his palm with the thick packet. "No, Ben, the times have turned on us and we're getting too old to turn with them."

"I can't accept it as easy as you, Walt. I'm thankful I'm not gonna be around long enough to see too much more of it. Shoot, in less than six months it's gonna be a new century. You ever think about that? We've outlived the old one. 1900! Gives me the shivers to think about it."

Devon's face clouded. "You learn to accept what life throws at you or you go under," he said.

The silence lingered, except for the rattle of dice in Harry's cell and the steady marching beat of the clock on the wall. Kraker knew this wasn't the time to bring it up, but he said it just the same.

"I heard about Ferro. I'm sorry."

Devon's head jerked around. The corner of his lips twitched. "That's the sort of thing I was referring to."

Then the telephone jingled. Kraker went to the wall and put the earpiece to his head. He frowned and said, "Where is she?"

Horschmann looked up from the dice. Devon tucked the transport papers into his inside vest pocket. Kraker said, "I'll be right there," and hung up the instrument.

"Trouble?" Devon asked.

"Trouble. You mind tending the store while I'm away?"

"Sure."

Kraker took the gun holster from a peg, strapped it around his waist and left.

THIRTEEN

CIGARETTE and coal oil smoke thickened the air and constricted Danny's throat. He shifted on the bench and felt for a splinter that speared his bottom. His fingers removed the offending sliver and Jake Tollar elbowed him when he glanced at the piece of wood. With lips pulled down, Danny resumed his vacant stare, his lungs heavy with foul air, while all around a crush of humanity waited to be saved and healed.

"Listen to me, good people, all you who are sick and heavy-laden with sin. You can have healing!" Justin Tollar's voice peaked. "Healing, I tell you, and you don't have to do nothing but believe. That's all! Believe and come forward. You got the gout? Arthy-ritus and rheumatism? You crippled or darkened of eyes? Does the misery dwell in your back or your lungs? Headaches, dyspepsia, bad teeth?" Tollar heaved in a long, rattling breath and dropped his voice to barely a whisper. "Then listen to me, fine people. There *is* healing for you. In the Word, in the Lord, if only you'll believe. Do I hear Amen?"

The crowd responded.

"Amen!" Tollar threw his arms towards the tent top, Bible clutched in his right hand, his left hand balled into a fist. "Hallelujah, brothers and sisters, I feel the spirit moving among us tonight!"

Danny didn't feel it, at least he didn't think he did. He only felt hot and choked and wicked. His mother had taken him to tent meetings before, but no preacher had ever made the bold claims that Justin Tollar had been proclaiming the last forty-five minutes. She would be horrified if she knew the charade he was to take part in. Thinking of her intensified his guilt. *Why did he allow Brad to talk him into coming to Cripple Creek in the first place?*

He chanced a sideways glance; Brad was peering straight ahead, as if hypnotized with Justin Tollar's robust voice, and he wasn't the only one entranced. Tollar's words had struck at the secret wants and desires of the crowd, had speared the heart of each of them. Their wills gathered in the palm of his hand—and he knew it!

A hush settled in the tent as the people quieted, together with Justin, to feel the Spirit move amongst them. Tollar allowed the pause to last just long enough, then in a more subdued voice said, "Sister Mercie will come forward now and lead us in a hymn of praise and thanksgiving while the plate is being passed and then we'll let the healing begin!"

Margaret Mercie had slipped quietly into the service from a flap in the back wall of the tent and had taken a chair discreetly off to one side of the raised platform. Now she stood, smiling sweetly and opening a tattered hymnal as she came to the front.

Danny tried to watch without appearing to be doing so. A boy about his own age appeared at the front of the platform carrying two deep wicker baskets. The boy started the baskets down the aisles. All at once Jake Tollar grabbed Danny's hand and stood up.

"Wait just one minute, mister," he said to Justin above a sea of craning necks and staring eyes. Jake had changed from his suit and vest of earlier to dark canvas pants and a dusty blue cotton shirt. He had tied a sweat stained bandanna about his neck and had smudged mine dust on his cheek. All and all, he looked much like every other man there. His hair needed a comb and his chin needed a shave and he probably just climbed out of the mines an hour or so earlier.

Margaret Mercie cut her song off in the middle of a hallelujah and Justin stood up tall and smiled over the heads of the congregation. "Brother, if something is not right here, please speak."

"Darn right I'll speak, padre. I've been sittin' here most of a hour now, listening to your fancy words, but I ain't seen no action!"

"Action?" Justin sounded perplexed. "Don't you feel the Spirit, brother, don't you know there will be miracles worked tonight?"

"I don't feel no Spirit. I ain't seen no healing neither. All I seen was a fancy preacher with fancy words making fancy promises. And now you're passing the collection plate before we seen any action!"

The crowd mumbled their agreement. Justin threw up his hands to quell the rebellion. "Fair enough, brother. I myself would not buy a hen until I'd seen it lay."

The crowd agreed.

"Nor would I buy a cow until I tasted her milk. Brother, some people have faith and see a miracle, others need a miracle to have faith. In your case, brother, you need the miracle first. So be it! I will show you a miracle so that you and everyone else here can believe! What is it you require of me?"

"Fair enough, reverend," Jake Tollar said, retreating from his challenging tones. "You show me a miracle and I'll fill your basket." He pulled a poke from his pocket and dangled it from its leather strap so that all could see. "I got seven ounces of gold here. You heal my boy and it's yours."

A murmur rippled through the crowd. It reached Justin and he smiled and nodded his head and accepted the challenge. He thrust his Lincoln-jaw up and said, "Father, we need us a mighty miracle tonight! A miracle like you made for Samson in the temple of Dagon of the Philistines! Like you done for Elijah, sending fire from heaven to consume the sacrifice on Mount Carmel!" Tollar's voice boomed. "Like the miracle that saved Daniel from the lion's den! Oh, perform such a miracle here tonight that the faithless will believe!" Justin Tollar bent over suddenly as if attacked by a case of stomach misery, then pulled himself up straight, heaving the rancid air into his lungs. A smile appeared on his face, as if a great peace had filled him, and he said softly, "So be it. Amen."

Danny dragged a finger under his shirt around his neck, thankful his mother hadn't forced him to add a collar to his discomfort, too. Now the eyes of the crowd were upon him and he gulped, pretending he didn't notice.

Justin said, "Bring the lad forward."

Jake sidestepped from the center of the pew to the aisle with Danny's wrist clamped tightly in his hand.

"What be his ailment?"

"Blind. Blind from from a accident in the mine."

"And how long has he been without sight?" Justin asked.

"Three years."

Danny tripped going up to the platform. He performed the charade well; his guilt rose higher. Justin took his other hand, helped him up the final step.

Justin went down on one knee to Danny's level and took him by the shoulders. "Son, now this ain't a gonna hurt you one bit, so don't be scared."

"I'm not."

"Good, good. Now I got to ask you a question and you answer me honestly."

"Yes, sir."

"Do you believe in the power of the Spirit? That there is healing in the Word."

He'd been instructed to answer "yes" and to say it loud enough for everyone to hear. He did and Justin announced to the crowd, "The boy has the faith and with faith nothing is impossible!"

He looked over their faces. "And if you want to be healed here tonight you, too, must have this faith, even as a little child."

A hornet's nest of anticipation began to stir. Justin rose again to his full height and laid a hand over Danny's eyes. He prayed loudly and forcefully and then his hand began to quiver. All at once he pulled his hand away and said, "It is done, Amen. The boy can see!"

"I can see!" Danny blurted, remembering to add a note of

excitement to his voice, just as Margaret Mercie had instructed him. Then Jake was swinging him up into his arms and giving him a huge hug. Then Jake pumped Justin's hand, pulled the heavy poke from his pocket and plopped it into the wicker basket. From then on the giving was free and generous and when the baskets reached the back of the tent the lad struggled with the burden of coins and dust to carry them forward.

Margaret finished her hymn. Justin made the call and folks clamored to the aisle. Brad moved into line near the front where Margaret said he needed to be. He was what she called "reinforcement," though neither he nor Danny had been certain what she meant by that.

Danny spied his brother third down from the front. He seemed preoccupied with the dirt beneath his shoes. Overhead the kerosene lanterns swayed on wire hooks as the people below flowed around the uprights. Jake hauled Danny back to their splintered bench. A lady with a bent back was just leaving the platform. Her back was still bent, but she seemed not to notice it now and was smiling. Reverend Tollar had told her she was healed. The man behind her didn't receive healing of his stiff knee, and Justin regretted his lack of faith and sent him back to his seat, admonishing him to pray about it.

The man grumbled and the crowd grumbled and Justin ignored them all and motioned for Brad to come up the steps. Justin asked the usual questions and laid his hand upon Brad's head. Danny couldn't stand the embarrassment. He looked away and his breath caught in his throat at the sight of the man that came through the tent flap and stopped just inside. The man didn't see Danny, but then he wouldn't have known him if he had, but Danny knew him! He also knew by the narrowing of his one good eye that the man recognized Brad right off.

Danny wanted to jump up and shout a warning, but it was too late. The healing had begun. In the back of the tent Malcolm Hollendorfer frowned, then grinned and scratched an itch under the black eye patch.

FOURTEEN

MILLER THOMPSON chewed the end of a dead cigar. Shreds of wet tobacco leaf clung to his drooping mustache. On his balding head sat a frayed, narrow-brimmed hat more the color of rock dust than silverbelly. His gray shirt was buttoned to the neck and a shapeless, black wool jacket hung from his shoulders.

Kenny Roberts looked much the same, minus the cigar and jacket. He wore dark overalls covered with the same fine-grain dust which coated everything that emerged from the mines.

Horschmann poured them each a drink and topped up his own glass. "Been a change of plans," he said, setting the bottle back on the table.

"I thought there was to be three of us, Bernie," Roberts said.

"There will be. Gardner's shift ends in half an hour."

Thompson removed the cigar and spit a fleck of tobacco leaf to the floor. "I heard there's a marshal in from Canon City to take Harry back with him. What about it?"

"What?" Roberts looked suddenly concerned. "You said it was just gonna be that old man we had to contend with."

Horschmann grinned at him. "Don't get too worked up over it, Kenny. From what I hear, that marshal is encroaching on antiquity himself."

"You don't grow old in his line of work if you ain't good," Roberts observed.

"Now ain't a good time to be getting cold feet," Horschmann said evenly.

"I ain't, Bernie. I just want to be certain you know what you're doing."

"You let the thinking up to me, and you take care of your end."

A slow grin moved across Kenny Robert's face. "It will be like shooting ducks at a carnival."

"I can vouch for that, Bernie," Thompson interjected. "Kenny here is good."

Roberts took a drink to hide a grin.

"What sort of change in plans?" Thompson asked.

Horschmann leaned forward. "They're taking Harry out early tomorrow morning. Before light. The two-forty train."

"Two-forty train?" Thompson thought a moment. "That's the train to Colorado Springs. Why to the Springs? The F&CC to Florence would drop them closer to Canon City than the Colorado Midland."

"Ain't you heard?" Roberts said. "The F&CC lost another bridge in Phantom Canyon last week. Be at least a week before they get the tracks open again."

Thompson said, "Someday they're gonna have one too many of those floods and never reopen that road."

"Not so long as they make money off it, and the F&CC makes a *lot* of money."

"Who's making a lot of money?" Stu Gardner pulled back a chair and sat down.

"We was talking about the Florence and Cripple Creek," Thompson said.

"Heard they lost another bridge last week."

"So we've just been discussing," Horschmann said. "Your shift ended early." He opened his watch.

"We're into a vein of soft rock. Had the charges set ahead of schedule. So, what was so urgent that Rheutters had to leave a message for me?"

Horschmann poured Gardner a drink. Stu Gardner was a short, powerfully built man of twenty-nine. He wore a cloth cap with a celluloid bill and dark overalls over a dark shirt. The bandanna around his sweaty neck had originally been red. Now it was the same brownish-gray color that streaked his cheeks and colored his hat—an indigenous color to Cripple Creek, like the blue of the sky and the green of the forested mountain slopes. No one took much notice of it.

"Just tidying up loose ends," Horschmann said.

"What loose ends?"

"A change in time, that's all. Instead of tomorrow morning, it will be earlier."

"How much?"

"A few hours."

"That still makes it tomorrow morning," Gardner observed, sampling Horschmann's whiskey. He found the taste to his liking and downed the whole glass.

"Two o'clock or so."

"Whew. No sleep tonight. Better fill me up again, Bernie."

Roberts chuckled and said, "Reckon you won't be spending any time with that new girl friend of yours tonight, Stu."

Gardner leveled a narrow eye at him. Cindy Ryan wasn't that kind of girl—but to admit to them the wholesomeness of their relationship would only bring upon him hoots of disbelief and lessen him in their eyes. He let the comment slide and looked back at Horschmann.

Horschmann grinned and clanked the bottle against the rim of the glass. "Now don't get too liquored up or you'll be worthless to me."

Thompson sucked the soggy end of his cigar contemplatively. "It'll be a good idea if we all lay off the booze until this is over."

Gardner tossed back the whiskey. "Miller's probably right. One more, Bernie, then we'll celebrate proper-like when this is all over. I've worked the graveyard with a hangover before, I reckon I can do it again tomorrow."

"I'll drink to that—we'll all drink to that," Horschmann said with a finality that invited no argument. He filled their glasses and raised his in a toast. "Success, gentlemen, and to my brother, Harry, who ain't got a lick of horse sense in his head."

"Success," they replied. Horschmann corked the bottle and set it back in the corner. Gardner came back from the bar with a bowl of roasted goobers and a brass cuspidor and immediately sliced a chew from his plug, pressing it between his cheek and teeth. Thompson lighted the stub of his cigar and made a face. He crushed it under his heel and stood, saying he needed a fresh smoke.

Roberts grabbed a fistful of goobers and cracked one between his teeth. He glanced back over his shoulder at the batwing door to see what had just attracted Horschmann's attention. It was Karl Rheutters, and he was carrying a rifle. He sat in Thompson's vacated chair and stood the rifle in the corner. His face telegraphed his excitement, which he found impossible to contain one moment longer.

"Spotted the kid, Bernie."

Horschmann's sodden eyes came to life. "Where?"

"Virge Amberly seen him go into that tent meeting they're having down by the depot. Fits the description, except he was hobbling on a crutch."

"A crutch? Is Virge certain?"

"Certain about the crutch, and he's near sure it's the same kid you're willing to pay five dollars to find."

Horschmann thought a moment and pushed back his chair. "Only one way to find out." Granger and Roberts followed along. Horschmann left the bottle and the rifle with the barkeep and on the way out picked up Miller Thompson on the front sidewalk, putting a match to a fresh cigar.

"Where we going in such a hurry?"

"Teach a nosey brat a lesson he ain't soon to forget." Horschmann grinned and they all seemed anxious to see what he had in mind.

* * *

Ben Kraker wheezed like a leaky boiler and a lump of granite was forming in his chest. He slowed to a brisk walk, and then just a walk. Ahead the knot of people that tightened around the sidewalk suddenly pulled apart and a pillar of orange flame spit into the night sky, followed a moment later by the thunder of a shotgun. Ben moved into a trot.

He shouldered through the onlookers. *Damn Denver doctor.* He took three calming breaths, but the lump of granite remained. The crowd had expanded into a wide circle. In the middle of the circle Grace DeVere wheeled and threatened to pull the second trigger. The double-barreled shotgun came down. Folks scrambled aside. Grace was stark naked.

"Grace," Kraker said. She and the shotgun came around. Kraker flinched in a moment of embarrassment, but he fixed his eyes upon her tortured face and spoke gently. "Give me the gun, Grace."

"Likes hell I'll give it up!" She leaned forward, squinted, staggered and caught her step. "Iss that you Ben Kraker?"

"Yes, Grace." He moved towards her, extended his hand.

"No, sir, yous ain't takin' aways from me this time, Ben Kraker." She leveled the weapon at his open vest.

Kraker was breathing deeply. His head swam. *Hell, who'd have thought a man could take in too much oxygen at this elevation!* He held his breath and felt his brain clear.

"Grace, you're drunk, and you're indecent. You might hurt someone."

"Drunk! Kraker, I ain't only drunk, I'm tiptoeing on clouds and I don't gives a tinker's damn. And as for indecent—" Grace looked down at herself, as if seeing the sagging pink flesh for the first time—"yous can blame Old Man Times for what he done to me, and that bastard J. D. Carpenter and his way with a razor. . . ." She looked at herself again, her wrinkled belly, her sagging breasts, the lumpy terrain of her hips. She blinked, her eyes glistened, her nose sniffed. "Men! They're all bastards! They want you when yous young and pretty, theys do, but when yous gets old they toss yous aside. Yous wants to know what's indecent? Mens whats indecent, Ben Kraker. Not this tired old body of mine."

"You can't change that, Grace. Don't make it any more

difficult than it already is. Give me the gun." His hand reached out.

"Don't force me to use this, Ben Kraker." Grace dug her toes into the dirt and manure of the street.

"You don't want to hurt anyone, Grace."

"That's where you am wrong. I wants to hurt everyone—everyone likes I'm been hurt." She swayed and stabbed a foot out to better anchor herself.

"You're only making matters worse. You know how you felt last week when you sobered up and learned you hit Alvin Leonard over the head with a dress form. Think how you'll feel if you kill someone."

"If'n I'm lucky I won't sober up."

"Grace, don't talk like that." Kraker advanced a step and stopped. Grace brought the butt of the shotgun to her shoulder. "Give the gun to me, Grace."

"No."

"Give me the gun." The hardness in the center of his chest settled to his stomach; he wanted to vomit. The people around him were charged with electricity. It filled the air. Fools, he thought. If that shotgun should go off—No, he could not allow that to happen. He swung for the long, blue barrel and Grace pulled the trigger.

Nothing happened. Her clouded brain wondered why and then, belatedly, realized her finger had tugged back on the forward trigger. The hammer to the left barrel was still cocked. She struggled to relocate the trigger finger, but Kraker wrenched up and away.

He wrapped an arm around Grace and pulled her to him, feeling only naked skin under his fingers. She fought him at first, then collapsed all at once, burying her face into his shoulder and sobbing. Kraker recoiled at the sickly odor of opium on her breath. He passed the shotgun to one of the men nearby and put the other arm about Grace in a fruitless attempt at modesty. "Someone find me a blanket," he said, then, "I'm sure you folks have something better to do than stand around gawking. Go on, get moving."

The circle fragmented into a dozen different directions

and someone handed Kraker a blanket. He wrapped Grace into it and with an arm around her waist helped her up the street. She went without a struggle, content to sob softly into the blanket, except for an occasional outburst of blue language when a bare foot came down on a sharp pebble or unnoticed road apple.

Kraker didn't speak, but thought about his breathing— *deep and regular*—to head off the sharp squeezing pains he knew lurked just around the corner.

* * *

Her husband's footsteps ascended the stairs and came into the bedroom. "Got the place all locked up for the night." He paused. "Why is the light turned down?"

"No, don't. Don't turn it up just yet."

"What are you doing?"

"Looking." Deirdre turned from the window, saw Charlie's large frame silhouetted in the door frame. He came to her and pulled back a corner of the light chintz curtains.

"Looking at what?"

She pointed at the two figures trudging up Bennett Avenue. "It's Grace DeVere again. This time she stripped down to her bare nothings and threatened to blow off Ben Kraker's head with a shotgun. The people appeared to be enjoying it. This town is a circus, Charlie."

"She brought it on herself," Charlie said coolly.

"Did she? Or maybe it was Cripple Creek that drove her to the water pipe and the liquor."

"No. The weakness is within her, Didi. Don't go trying to find someone else to carry the blame for the way a person behaves. Everyone is responsible for their own actions. Come away from that window and let's go to bed."

Deirdre sighed and let the curtain fall back in place. "Grace wasn't like that five years ago. Oh, she used to drink a little. That was all. Opium is more recent. Ever since her sister, Pearl—"

"Where did you know Grace DeVere from?"

A rush of blood colored Deirdre's cheeks. "Oh, we've met on occasion. And then, I have been in her dress shop." She added quickly. "I never bought anything, of course, never could afford it. But she seemed a nice person to talk to."

Charlie studied her in the faint glow of the lamplight. "I didn't know you knew her," he said with a hint of concern in his voice.

"Well, that was a long time ago. Before you came to work the mines, Charlie." Deirdre made it sound as if it were nothing.

"Back when you were a typesetter at the Cripple Creek *Crusher?*"

"Yes. The year they went out of print, the year I met you, Charlie, remember?"

"You were working at the Emporium, on Myers Avenue, when I met you."

"I had to do something to keep body and soul together," Deirdre came back pointedly. "I'd just lost one job; you couldn't expect me to get along on my good looks now, could you!"

Charlie took her by her shoulders. "I'm sorry, Didi. It's just that when I hear you talking about people like Grace or her sister, Pearl, as if you personally know them, well, it bothers me."

She turned out of his grasp and looked down on the busy street. Pools of illumination from the lighted shop windows turned the night into day. Ben Kraker and Grace were no longer in sight, but the image of Grace, naked and drugged and threatening the world with her shotgun, haunted Deirdre. *That could have been me.*

"What's wrong, Didi?"

"Nothing." She walked across the bedroom unbuttoning her dress, opened the wardrobe and took a hanger down from the bar.

"I didn't mean to upset you, Didi." Charlie closed the curtains and turned up the light. He watched his wife slip out of the dress and hang it carefully in the wardrobe.

Didi unbuttoned her undergarment, aware of movement behind her. Lamplight shadowed, then brightened the back of the wardrobe, where it glinted briefly off the shiny brass receiver of Charlie's old Winchester. Then the light shadowed again and Charlie came up behind her, his hands dropped lightly upon her hips. They slid up her waist and cupped her breasts. A warm rush swept over her and she hugged his hands to her, then freed herself of him and the remainder of her clothes whispered to the floor around her feet.

Later, Didi buried her face in her husband's shoulder. A warm tear moistened his skin, but he slept on contentedly. She thought of Grace, and of Pearl DeVere. They had both been good to her when she had first come to Cripple Creek, alone, five years ago. Pearl died of morphine, and Grace was well on her way to doing the same with opium.

Didi thought of the man sleeping beside her, her good fortune in finding such a man. She closed her eyes, feeling the comfort of his body against hers, but sleep did not come and, after an hour of waiting she knew it wouldn't—and she knew why. . . .

FIFTEEN

WHEN MILO JOHNSON RETURNED Devon was sitting at Ben's desk. "Where is Ben?" Milo asked.

"Trouble, I gathered. He spoke to someone on the telephone and left in a hurry. Now that you're back to watch over things, I think I'll go down the street and take another look around."

"Probably a good idea. I found Kern McDonald and Frank Sayers, but there was no way to get in touch with Lew Mattsen without sending a rider out to his brother's place. They haven't got the telephone wires strung out his way yet."

"I have a feeling that won't be too far off."

"Nope." Milo settled himself behind the type-writing machine again and looked at it. "Can't stop progress, and we seem to be getting more than our share of it up here, the real new stuff, I'm talking about, marshal. It's all the money; men strike a vein and become rich overnight. Guess they got to spend all that newfound wealth on something."

Ben Kraker came through the door. "Give me a hand here, Walt."

Grace DeVere had passed out. Kraker wrestled her through the doorway and handed Milo the shotgun. Devon put an arm around Grace's waist, slung one of her arms over his shoulder.

"Let's get her to one of the cots in there," Ben said, nodding towards the cells. Milo leaped ahead of them and pulled a barred door open.

"That's Grace DeVere," Milo said, surprised.

"In the flesh," Kraker replied with a weary smile.

Devon looked at Ben with concern showing. "What's the matter, Ben?"

"Shoot, Walt, you're worse than a mother hen."

Devon pulled back the chair for him and Kraker lowered himself into it, breathing a long, deep sigh. "Somedays I wonder why I do it."

"You need to slow down, Ben."

"Hell, don't you think I know that?"

"Can I get you something, Ben?" Milo asked.

"No, I just need to sit here a bit and rest. Thanks."

Harry Horschmann leaned through the bars of his cell. "I think that old man is sick."

Kraker shot a glance at him. "I still got enough vinegar to put you to bed and you know it."

"All right, Ben," Devon intervened softly. "You do look all done in. Why don't you catch a couple hours of rest? There is no reason you need to sit up these next few hours. Milo can take care of the place."

"Yeah, Ben, I'll watch over things, and McDonald and Sayers will be in soon."

Kraker perked up. "You found them?"

"It weren't no problem finding them, Ben. They were both home with their families."

"Good. How about Mattsen?"

"We'll need to send a rider out for him."

Kraker thought a moment. "That won't be necessary. The five of us should be sufficient. Don't you think, Walt?"

"We'll make out with what we have, Ben. Always have, haven't we?"

Kraker grinned. "That's the truth."

"What happened to her?"

"Too much whiskey and opium," he said, frowning. "Her name is Grace Devere; she owns a dress shop. It's a reputable business, the first she's been in, from what I gathered. Her sister was one of the more prominent madames in town until her death a couple of years back. Grace had been a silent partner in the brothel. After her sister died, she sold out her share and opened the shop on Bennett Avenue. She has always been a heavy drinker, but lately she started hitting the hookah. She is strung out most all the time now, and the opium seems to bring out a violent side to her nature. Last week she took to beating folks over the head with a dress form. The week before that she paraded up and down Bennett Avenue in her underwear, cussing out the local gentry. Tonight she stripped down to her birthday suit and punched a hole in the sky with that ten-gauger."

Devon glanced at the shotgun atop Milo's desk. "A stout gun for the little lady."

"They tell me it nearly set her on her can when she let go with the first barrel."

Devon went to the open cell and peered down at her. In the next cell over Harry stopped rattling the dice.

"Hey, marshal, why don't you peel back them covers and let me have a peekaboo?"

Devon looked at him. "What happened to your face?"

"He slipped and fell," Kraker said, peering over his cluttered desk at them.

"I'll bet." Devon studied a poker-faced Ben Kraker, then swung back to Horschmann. "Best watch yourself, son. Life in one of Ben Kraker's cells can be downright dangerous to your health." He turned to leave, stopped and looked back at Horschmann. "I haven't seen your brother about."

"He'll be here, old man, don't you worry about that. He'll come."

Devon grinned at him. "You're the one who ought to be worrying, boy."

"You taking off again?" Kraker asked when Devon snatched his hat from the desk.

"Thought I'd take another turn around the town. Does Miss DeVere have any friends—lady friends?"

"A few, I reckon. Only one comes to mind at the moment."

"It might be comforting if there was a lady here with her when she comes around."

"Yeah, you're probably right, Walt. But her friend, she's a
. . . er, what I mean to say is, her friend works nights."

Devon's eyes crinkled. "You want me to roust her out of
bed for you, Ben?"

"No, I can call on the telephone."

Devon viewed the box on the wall narrowly. "I keep forgetting about those things." He grinned. "I can see where
they'd be mighty handy, especially now. Least the talker on
the other end can't see your red face through that mouth
horn."

"Nope, and I hope man never gets that clever either."

"I hope not too, Ben." Devon put his hat on his head and
left.

He was grateful to be free of the confines of the heavily
pine-scented jail house, out again, striding along in the fresh
mountain air. The crisp night air brought a surge of vitality
to his step. He headed down into the heart of Cripple Creek
among the bustle of folks out after dark. Although Bennett
Avenue was still a busy place, it appeared almost deserted
compared to the night life only one block down. Devon
turned a corner and stopped on the corner of Myers Avenue
just as a brightly colored electric trolley car went rattling by,
clanging its bell.

He shouldered among the throng of miners, passed one
gaily lit saloon after another. Music from a dozen different
directions filled the street and further down another trolley
clanged its bell as it plucked passengers out of the press like
a passing fishing schooner.

Even the one-girl cribs tucked up Poverty Gulch were lit
up and doing a brisk business. A train rattled over the trestle
above their shanties and somewhere up an alley a string of
firecrackers erupted.

Devon bumped and sidestepped his way down Myers Avenue, turned into a saloon where he found some elbow room
and bought a drink. In a corner a piano played and a gal
dressed in huge feathers sang out of tune. After listening a
while, Devon decided the piano was out of tune, too, and he
wasn't even certain the piano player and the singer were

working on the same song, but the miners were well-oiled. They didn't care.

He left the saloon and its dubious entertainment and fought his way up to Third Street, turned the corner and was all at once alone. He climbed the steep incline back towards Bennett Avenue, leaving the confusion of Myers Avenue behind him, its noise still ringing in his ears, dulling his senses, so that he was only faintly aware of the odor of smoke moving on the wind.

* * *

Brad Medford's head was in a whirl. His nostrils stung of coal oil fumes and when he looked out over the expectant faces a cold sweat pricked his forehead. Second thoughts had already become massive doubts and he was certain that any moment he'd slip up and expose the ruse and himself. His head was light and floating and he wondered if his discomfort was as obvious to the people watching as it was to him. No, he reassured himself, remain calm and soon it would be all over.

Justin Tollar asked him the questions and mechanically he recited the proper answers. As Tollar finished speaking, another voice rang out from the front of the tent. Its familiar timbre brought Brad's startled face about with a snap.

"Fraud! Fraud!" The eye patch was a black spot on his ruddy face and he shook a handless stump at the canvas ceiling.

Tollar brought the crowd under control. "Brother, if you have a grievance—" he said.

"Don't you *brother* me, you cheating charlatan." Malcolm Hollendorfer bulled through the line of people and stopped with one foot on the platform step, his finger pointed in Tollar's reddening face. "You're trying to cheat these people. You're no more a healer than I am. You've profaned the Word of God and you've stolen their money."

Brad saw Tollar's anger rising like steam in a pressure cooker. His tall, lean body began to quiver like a volcano ready to heave forth fiery destruction, but Malcolm Hollendorfer only leaned closer. "That boy ain't a cripple!" His accusing finger shifted, stood poised in front of Brad's nose.

The mumbling of the crowd behind him increased. "Is that true?" a lady's voice sounded above the rest.

Hollendorfer turned towards them. "Not two hours ago I played poker with that boy in the Golden Charm Saloon and he could walk just as fine as you or I."

"How about it, Tollar?" someone shouted.

"Hey, kid, is that true?"

"I want my money back," another said.

In the whirl of confusion and heated words Brad discovered he was thinking of something else. His grandfather's watch wasn't visible in Hollendorfer's vest pocket, but there was a lump in his shirt pocket. Could it be there?

Someone came up on the platform. Tollar took a step backwards. A hand clamped Brad's shoulder. People flowed up and around them with angry voices and confused, unrecognizable words. A face appeared, demanding the truth. Brad's world flipped and fluttered like a suffocating fish on a muddy bank. He swung around with the crutch, knocked someone aside, felt wood and bone collide and made a mad dash for the back of the tent. Margaret Mercie was there to block his escape from the rear flap and he wheeled about and headed for the main door.

"Catch that boy," a man cried, hands grappling and missing. Brad saw Danny leaping from his seat and then in the doorway he saw someone else and his blood went cold. His thinking clouded further. Hands stabbed out and he sidestepped and rushed for his brother.

Out the corner of his eye he saw a half-dozen men tackle Justin Tollar and more scrambling out the back way after Margaret Mercie. Jake Tollar had made it out the front way, slipping past the stocky, red-haired man standing there.

"Danny!" They came together as the flood of people shifted and spread towards them. The center support cracked under their weight and the tent caved in. Kerosene lamps shattered and the angry screams turned to panic.

Danny threw his arms around Brad and they rolled under a bench as the canvas collapsed.

The sheets of canvas roiled like a fishing net, filled with the trapped people blinded by fear and the smoke that seeped under the material as sections turned brown, then yellow, and burst into flames.

Under the bench Brad and Danny watched the entanglement of legs, the trampling of bodies, felt the growing heat as a second lantern brought flames to another section of billowing canvas. Then the bench was kicked over and a suffocating shroud of canvas came down on them.

"Brad—"

Someone tripped over them.

Brad dug his fingers tighter into his brother's arm, fearing Danny would be swept along with the wave of humanity trying to find a way out.

Danny's hand suddenly appeared, holding a penknife. Brad snatched it away, opened it and stuck the point through the canvas, slicing a long, ragged opening. They poked their heads through. Cool air filled their lungs. Scrambling through, Brad pulled Danny out and they staggered across the bucking sheets, across the heads and bodies of those still trapped below. Flames leaped up in two separate places, spreading violently. Other people were cutting their way out of the tent, but only a few. The majority beat their way through the fallen-in opening, while some other lucky ones managed to wiggle under the sides where it had been staked to the ground. But, for the rest, the fiery tomb was spreading and there would be no escape.

Brad and Danny made it to safe ground. In the distance came the first clanking sounds of the fire wagon, but Brad knew it would be too late in arriving for those still trapped in that blazing inferno. Flames brightened the night sky and reflected orange and red against the tall Midland Terminal a short distance away.

"Let's get out of here," Brad said. He took Danny's hand and started towards Bennett Avenue, then stopped abruptly.

Bernard Horschmann saw him at that same instant. Brad swung away in a run, with Danny in tow.

Horschmann gave a signal to the others and they divided to head the boys off.

Brad tugged Danny into a dark alley and pounded towards a rectangle of light at the far end. Two men appeared. His heart thumping, his breath coming in short, burning gasps, Brad pulled Danny up short and reversed directions. Two other men were there also. Brad sniffed back the tears, desperately trying to rein in his emotions. These weren't kids playing games. They were grown, dangerous men, men he knew wanted to hurt or even kill him! He hugged Danny protectively to himself and wished he had never heard of this hell town called Cripple Creek!

Then the four men were close enough for Brad to see Bernard Horschmann clearly. Terror yanked his eyes wide when the razor-sharp knife flicked open.

SIXTEEN

THE BREEZE that ruffled the curtains carried with it a faint odor of smoke; a foreboding heaviness further depressed her, unbridled her thoughts and drove away sleep, bringing glimpses of her past before her eyes like pictures in an album.

Why did they have to knuckle under to the likes of Bernard Horschmann? she wanted to know. Her father wouldn't have buckled. But that was unfair. Her father was a different breed of man than Charlie. He'd come out to Colorado before the Indian trouble, fought through it and remained on the land. He was a fighter and, yes, she had some of that headstrong blood in her veins, too.

Perhaps, she rationalized, it was that fight within her that allowed her to take the kind of job Pearl and Grace DeVere had to offer when she had arrived in Cripple Creek, penniless and too proud to return home. She thought of the man sleeping next to her. How she wanted to keep that portion of her past hidden from him. She watched the chintz curtains rippling in the breeze, aware of Charlie's warm breath on the back of her shoulder. She should have been warm and content beneath the covers . . . but she couldn't sleep.

The clanking bell and pounding hoofbeats of the city pumper turning out of the firehouse, three buildings away, was finally too much. Deirdre gently disengaged herself from Charlie's heavy arms and slipped out of bed, naked in the faint light off the street. She shivered and pushed her arms through the sleeves of a flannel robe, tying it in front. When she lifted the sash and peered out, craning her neck, she was unable to see what was burning, but the odor of smoke was heavy and yellow and red light leaped and danced upon the brick wall of the depot at the head of the street. Distantly she heard the cries and screams. She pulled her head in and shut the window.

Hugging herself as if suddenly chilled, Deirdre paced the little room, glanced unhappily at the wall clock and stopped in front of the wardrobe to look down at the rumpled bulk of covers heaving softly. Quietly, with a glance over her shoulder to detect any stirrings from her husband, she opened the wardrobe and moved her neatly hanging dresses aside. Back in the corner stood Charlie's old '73 Winchester; in the faint light its brass receiver seemed to glow and beckon to her.

"No," she whispered firmly, turning abruptly away and viewing her husband's sleeping form. Why did she feel she was betraying him? Wasn't she really betraying herself?

She closed the wardrobe. It was useless now to try to sleep, and Deirdre was a realist when it came to such things. If she were a drinking woman, she might have poured herself a glass of whiskey and allowed the liquor to take away her problems. Not so inclined, she instead turned to her only real vice and removed from a shelf the book she'd purchased the previous day on the recommendation of a friend.

She moved the chair to the window and struck a match. Charlie stirred, then settled down to even breathing. Deirdre turned up the lamp slightly and opened the book. It was written by an Englishman and she wondered if Mr. Wells's flight of fantasy into the far future could carry her away from her present dark mood.

She read the first sentence. *"The Time Traveller (for so it will be convenient to speak of him) was expounding on a recondite matter to us."* Time travel? What a perfectly marvelous idea!

The hands of the clock traveled past the tenth hour and advanced on towards the eleventh.

* * *

Kenny Roberts threw an arm around Danny and lifted him off the ground. "What you want me to do with this one, Bernie?"

Bernard Horschmann couldn't be bothered with the kid. "Just hang onto him till we finish here."

"All right, but hurry it up. He's a squirmin' handful."

"Then slug him!"

"Aw, he's only a kid. I can handle him."

Horschmann was anxious to be finished before someone wandered up the alleyway. Miller Thompson had Brad by the right arm, Stu Gardner had his left arm and a hank of hair in his fist, pulling Brad's head back to expose the smooth skin of his gulping throat. Rheutters watched, grinning.

The knife played back and forth in the darkness, catching and reflecting the distant light from up on Bennett Avenue. Brad's eyes followed it like a cobra under the spell of a charmer.

"Boy, no one never taught you to keep your snotty nose out of other people's affairs, huh?" Horschmann touched the point of the blade to his throat.

Brad recoiled from the cold metal. Their hands tightened around his arms. Earlier, when Horschmann had come at him with a knife, he had been able to move, to fight back. Now, helpless, he saw no hope for escape. He thought of the wrinkled and yellowed newspaper clipping in his pocket. *The Denver Post* never warned him of Cripple Creek's dark side. Oh, it had hinted at it, left-handedly, while waving the carrot of the Myers Avenue resorts in front of his face, but it never told him a person could end up dead in a back alley.

"What about it? You make a habit of sticking your nose where it don't belong? You're not talking so big now, kid."

"I . . . I'm sorry," Brad croaked, as if that could make a difference.

"I'll just bet you are, but it's a little too late for that." The blade was razor sharp and Brad hardly felt it prick the skin under his jaw and slice it down to the collar bone. He cried out and warm blood trickled down his chest. Thompson put a hand over his mouth.

"Please, mister," Danny pleaded.

"Shut that brat up!" Horschmann turned back to Brad. "Now, see just how pretty I can carve you up, boy? Neater than a holiday turkey—"

Kenny Roberts let out a cry. In the darkness something fell to the ground. Horschmann's head came around. Roberts was fanning his hand as if to free it of a swarm of bees.

"He bit me! The little bastard bit me!"

"Get him!"

Roberts turned after Danny, but in the dark he caught the tip of his boot under the downspout of a rain gutter and plunged headlong into the gravel. He sat up, cursing, with the gravel's hot sting in his face and arms. Danny turned up another alley and was gone.

"We better get out of here," Gardner said.

Roberts got to his feet and trudged back, brushing his pants and shirt.

"Not till I'm done!" Horschmann growled, turning purposefully back to Brad.

* * *

Devon stopped and sniffed the air. Now that the din of Myers Avenue was behind him, he became aware of a different sort of commotion coming from the street above. Ahead, through the pools of light up on the corner, people rushed on as if one side of the town had been tilted up and they were all tumbling uncontrollably towards the opposite end. The odor of smoke he had thought he smelled earlier now settled heavily about him and a shift in the wind brought a gray-black cloud over the tops of the buildings.

He'd been thinking of his son, Ferro, never comforting thoughts these days, and he was thankful for a reason to put them aside. He quickened his steps when a small, dark shape suddenly exploded from the alley and crashed headlong into his chest.

"What the dickens!" Devon staggered back a step and

took the object in hand, which turned out to be a boy. "Son, you ought to watch where you—" Then he recognized him.

Danny looked up and up at Devon. Up past the gun belt, past the black wool vest and red bib-front shirt, up to the craggy leather face he remembered from the train.

The wide hat shadowed Devon's eyes. They narrowed. "What's wrong, son. Where is your brother?" Somehow he knew Brad was in danger—Danny's eyes proclaimed it loudly, even thought his tongue was having difficulty coordinating the words. "Settle down, boy. Tell me what happened."

"They're gonna kill him, they're gonna kill my brother!" Danny blurted between his gulps of air and the tears he could no longer control.

"Who's going to hurt him?"

"Some men. I don't know who they are, but they have a knife!"

"Show me where, boy."

Danny wheeled back into the alley. Devon followed, but Danny outdistanced him and turned a dark corner ahead. Devon's lungs burned in the thin air as he lengthened his stride. As he neared the corner and heard the sounds of a struggle.

He came around and stopped, assessing the scene in a single glance. Two men held Brad against the wall, while a third was doing something to him. The glint of light off steel was all Devon could be certain of in the darkness. Danny had launched himself into a swinging-kicking battle with a fourth man. Devon didn't wait to see any more.

* * *

Kenny Roberts saw Devon first, but he had the kid all over him. No time for that now. He backhanded Danny, sending him sprawling into the building across the alley. "Trouble!" he called over his shoulder, turning to swing a fist.

Devon came down on him like a wounded grizzly. The thirty years in age that separated the two men made little difference. He parried Roberts's attack and grabbed up a handful of shirt, lifting him off the ground. His right hand balled into knuckles and shot out like the driving piston of a locomotive; a short, powerful jab that crumpled Roberts instantly. Devon tossed him aside.

The remaining men gave ground and Brad slumped to his knees.

"Get him," Horschmann said, shoving Miller Thompson forward.

Thompson wasn't so sure. He was taller than the rest of them, but the old man coming at him topped him by a good half-a-head and his bunched shoulders spanned twice the distance of Thompson's own shoulders—or at least that was his impression. "We can take him together—" he began to say when he realized all at once that he was alone. Gardner, Rheutters, and Horschmann were receding rapidly up towards Bennett Avenue. Miller turned to join them when a hand came down on his shoulders and spun him about. A fist expanded in his field of vision . . . and then there was only blackness.

SEVENTEEN

"BRAD, Brad, are you all right?"

Devon drew up. They were on the run and he was too old to catch them in a foot race. Behind him Danny's voice pleaded with his older brother to *please be all right!* Devon bent over Brad.

"Is he dead?" Danny cried.

"No, only fainted. They worked him over some, but it doesn't appear they intended to kill your brother—at least not right off. We need to get him out of here."

A groan came from up the alley. Devon drew his pistol and helped Kenny Roberts to his feet. "Let's see if we can't wake your friend," he said, poking the gun barrel into Roberts's spine. Kenny staggered over to where Thompson lay and went to his knees.

"Miller, come on, Miller, get up." His words slurred through thickening lips. He looked up helplessly at Devon.

"Keep trying, I didn't hit him that hard."

"Hey, Miller, wake up."

Thompson's eyes fluttered. He rolled over, coughing up blood. It flowed freely from his crushed nose and Devon tossed him a handkerchief. "Get to your feet."

"I can't. I'm hurt bad."

"Not as bad as you're gonna be if you don't hurry it up."

Thompson's eyes stopped on the pistol that had jerked in Devon's hand. "Yes . . . yes, sir." He stood unsteadily.

"Marshal," Danny said urgently. "Brad is waking up!"

"Help your brother to his feet and we'll haul this crowd down to Ben Kraker's jail."

Ben wasn't there when Devon escorted his two prisoners through the front door, but Milo Johnson was, and so were two other men.

"Where's Ben?"

"He was rousted out of bed not ten minutes after he laid down. Damn fire down by the tent meeting. I told Ben I'd take care of it, but he would have none of that. What you got here?"

"Assault and attempted murder. Lock them up."

"Kenny . . . Miller? What happened to you two?" Harry Horschmann was at the bars.

"You know these two yahoos?" Devon said.

"Yeah, I know 'em."

"Ben might be interested in hearing that," Devon said to Milo.

"I'll let him know."

Danny helped Brad into Kraker's chair.

"What happened to that one?"

Devon said, "Those two and some others were working him over with a shiv. Better call a doctor."

"Right." Milo went to the telephone, cranked the handle.

The door opened and Crystal Lane stepped in.

"Where's Grace?" she asked urgently and then saw Brad. "Oh!" She blinked up at Devon. "What happened to him?"

"It was those men, ma'am," Danny said. "The ones that tried to hurt you earlier. Them and some others."

Crystal put a gloved hand on Brad's head and her mouth drew into a tight line. "Damn!" she said under her breath. And then, with sudden resolution in her voice, "Where is the police chief?"

"Out to the fire, ma'am," Milo said.

"I want to file a complaint against Bernard Horschmann," she said firmly.

"I can take care of that."

Harry Horschmann was at the bars, startled, but he said nothing. Devon grinned at him. "Looks like you'll be having more company in there."

Harry glared. "You still don't have him, old man."

"Maybe not, but now with a warrant out for his arrest he may have more important things on his mind than planning a break for his little brother."

"Not Bernie," Harry said confidently. "Bernie won't let you take me, old man."

Devon looked at the clock. "Well, another few hours will tell."

Ben Kraker chose that moment to step through the door, shaking his head. "Terrible thing," he was saying when he noticed the two boys. Crystal Lane was seated by Milo's desk and the jail cell bulged with extra prisoners. He stopped, held himself straight with some effort and looked questioningly at Devon.

Devon shrugged his shoulders. "I just went out for a walk, Ben."

"Suppose you tell me about it, Walt," Kraker replied wearily, dropping his hat on a hook.

* * *

Crystal finished filing the complaint and said to Kraker, "I feel terrible about poor Brad. If I'd done this earlier—when you first asked it."

"Can't undo what's been done." He squinted at her signature, then folded the paper and slid it into an inside pocket of his vest.

Crystal looked down at herself, then folded her hands resolutely in front of her. "I'm afraid there's more truth to that than you know, Mr. Kraker."

Ben heard the inflection in her voice and decided against comment. This was no time for fatherly advice from an old man she'd only met for the first time a few hours ago. "I'm glad you were able to come," he said instead.

Crystal smirked. "You were afraid I'd be busy?"

Ben reddened at her frankness. "Well, as a matter of fact, ma'am, yes, I was."

"Normally I would have been. I had an appointment scheduled that never showed." She looked sadly at Brad. Brad had regained consciousness now and was stretched out on a cot with the doctor bent over him. Crystal didn't mention who her appointment had been with. "Oh, well, it was probably for the best," she continued with a sigh. "I'd better go to Grace now, before she wakes up."

Kraker stepped aside for her, glanced unhappily at Devon, then joined Doc Willis.

"How's the boy?"

Danny knelt by Brad's head and peered up at Kraker. Behind Kraker, Devon towered over him, looking over his shoulder.

Willis said, "The boy will be fine. Lots of cuts but nothing serious. I'd like to get him over to my place. He's going to need stitches."

"I'll have McDonald and Sayers give you a hand with him, Doc."

Willis cleared his throat. "Ah . . . I have to know who is going to cover it, Mr. Kraker?"

"Cover it? You mean who's to foot the bill?"

Willis nodded his head.

"Hell, send the bill to the city. They can afford it. The boy's an orphan, after all!" Kraker looked sharply at Danny. "Ain't that right, boy?"

Danny's face whitened. He didn't reply.

Kraker nodded for Devon to follow him and they went to the cluttered desk. He sat in the chair and peered regretfully at the cot he had vacated at the news of the fire. "Turning into quite a night, Walt."

Devon remained silent, studying Kraker with a concerned eye.

"Aw, don't look at me like that. Sometimes I work clear through the night."

"Not recently, I'll wager."

Kraker grinned. "No, probably not. But I'll be all right. I'm better off than fifteen poor souls down at that tent meeting. They're in no need of healing now."

"Bad?"

Kraker nodded his head. "There is at least a dozen more burned real bad. Fifteen died and and at least that many more took in enough smoke to gag a locomotive. Coroner is there now with his staff and the fire department. Shoot, I was just getting in the way. Apparently the preacher was a carpetbagger and got away when the tent caved in. And we still have another problem, Walt."

"Bernard Horschmann."

"Now that I have a signed complaint, I can haul him in, except he probably knows that. He'll be harder to flush now."

"That can work in our favor. He'll stay low if he knows he's being hunted. Maybe forget about his little brother, try to save his own hide."

Kraker frowned. "I wouldn't count on that."

"Then I better take another stroll around town." Devon stood.

"If you want I'll send McDonald and Sayers around after you when they get back from the doc's place."

"That won't be necessary, Ben. You keep them here with you. Let them know what we're planning. Besides, if brother Bernard gets bold, he might try the jail and you'll need the extra guns."

"Perhaps. You watch yourself, Walt."

Devon tugged his hat onto his head. "Watching myself is something I'm good at, Ben. See you in a little bit." He went out the door, into the evening air and started back down the long hill into Cripple Creek's churning bowel. He didn't really expect to find Horschmann. He'd be lying low now, knowing Brad would identify him and there'd be a warrant out for his arrest. But Devon kept his eye open for him just the same, although his primary concern was the dark building tops, the blackened windows and shadowed alleyways that opened onto Bennett Avenue at regular intervals.

A cold finger ran up Devon's spine . . . or maybe it was only a gust of mountain air sliding down into the valley from the chilled, black peaks that pressed against the starry sky.

* * *

Bernard scooted down the tailing slope on the seat of his pants, reached the bottom and made his way to the shadows of a corrugated tin hoist shack. From out of the darkness came the sound of crunching gravel and in a moment a black form appeared and joined him. Stu Gardner fell against the building, rattling the metal and drawing deep gulps of the thin air into his lungs.

"I . . . I don't think he followed us," Gardner said between breaths.

The hoist rigging cross-hatched the sky, the brighter, moonlit clouds behind it sharpening the black lines of the cables and the skyward thrust of the uprights.

Horschmann said, "Who the hell was that guy, anyway?"

"I don't know, Bernie. Haven't seen him before."

Horschmann stared at the pattern the black cables made against the clouds. "Well, it ain't important." The breeze carried with it the odor of smoke. The orange glow that had resided over the building tops of the town below was no longer visible. Horschmann looked towards Cripple Creek and said, "I'm going to have to stay here a while. That kid knows me. The minute I set foot in town, Kraker will have his men all over me. But the kid doesn't know you."

"No, but Thompson and Roberts know me and they're in Ben Kraker's jail."

"They won't talk."

"Maybe not, Bernie, but I'd just as soon keep low, too, if it's all the same to you."

"We'll still have to go back to spring Harry."

Gardner looked at him. "You aren't still planning to do that now, are you, Bernie? It's crazy. Kraker will have men looking for us!"

"I ain't gonna let them take Harry! I'll spring him, then head out for somewhere—maybe California. We were going to California when Cripple Creek pulled us away."

"You got a good racket here, Bernie."

"*Had* a good racket. What do you think it will be worth once I kill the police chief and a marshal? The state will send troopers in and clean us out. No, once we spring Harry, it's good-bye Colorado. You'd better make plans, too."

Gardner sat back. "I don't know, Bernie. I kinda like it here."

"There are other places."

"Why don't you let 'em take Harry? That way we can keep what we have. This thing with the boy will blow over. Worse to happen is they'll slap your wrist, maybe throw us in jail for a few weeks. Then we can put things back together the way they were."

"No. I'm not gonna let Harry rot away in some prison."

"Why the hell not? He's never done you much good. It was because of him you had to leave Pennsylvania. Now you gonna leave Colorado. Keep him around too long, Bernie, and you'll soon run out of states."

"He's my brother, damnit. Now I don't want to hear no more about it!"

"What's that?" Gardner came suddenly alert at the sound of movement in the darkness beyond the pile of mine tailings.

Bernard peeked around the hoist shack. Moonlight paled through long, gray fingers of a cloud drift. He whistled and waved his arm. A man stopped abruptly, then trotted over to the shack.

"So, this is where the two of you got off to," Karl Rheutters said, dropping down on his haunches. "The way you hightailed it out of there, I figured you'd be halfway to Kansas by now." His grin broadened. "Hell, that wasn't but an old man back there."

"A *big* old man," Gardner said ruefully, "and maybe you best tell that to Thompson and Roberts. They sure didn't slow up that *old man* when he came on."

"I didn't see you waiting around to take him on," Horschmann noted.

Rheutters looked at the rubble at his boots. "I guess I just got caught up in your suddenness. Shoot, I stopped after fifty paces and went around to see what was going on."

"What'd you see?"

"Nothing more than I expected. That marshal rounded

up Thompson and Roberts and hauled them off to jail. The kid was making it under his own power."

"Marshal?" Horschmann looked startled. "You mean that's the man who's taking Harry?"

"Shoot, yeah, Bernie. You didn't know?"

"I'd never seen him before."

"Boyd Rawlin pointed him out to me earlier. He didn't tell you?"

"You were there when I talked to Rawlin."

"I left before you finished," Rheutters reminded him.

"He told me. Only I never seen him."

"Well, now you have," Rheutters said, grinning.

"Yeah, now I have," Horschmann repeated. "And I say there have been too many people poking their noses into my business today."

"What you going to do about it, Bernie?" Rheutters asked.

"The same thing I started out to do, only I'm going to be damned sure when the shooting starts that the marshal is sitting in my rifle sight."

"Now you're talking, Bernie."

Horschmann looked at Rheutters. "We're going to need another gun. Go back into town and find Boyd Rawlin for me and make sure he has a rifle with him. Then stop off at the Exchange and pick up my rifle. Meet us back here. I don't want to show my face around town until it's time."

Karl Rheutters left and Horschmann settled back into the shadows to wait. Stu Gardner wasn't happy but he knew this wasn't the time to voice his disapproval, so he found a place to sit and wait. That gave him time to think. Cindy Ryan crept into his thoughts, and the more he thought about her, the surer he became that he really didn't want to leave Cripple Creek because of the Horschmann brothers.

EIGHTEEN

DOCTOR WILLIS examined his handiwork as a painter might stand back and eye a canvas. "After those stitches come out," he said finally, "you'll hardly see where they cut you."

"It's simply awful what some folks are capable of doing," Betsy Willis stated, shaking her head. She gathered up the needles and sutures and deposited them in a white porcelain bowl by the sink. When she came back, she put a hand on Brad's shoulder. "How are you feeling now?"

"Better," Brad replied, cautiously touching the bandage under his jaw. Betsy helped him thread an arm through his shirt sleeve and pull it over his shoulder.

Willis came back, drying his hands. "What did you do to those fellows to make them so angry?"

Brad shrugged his shoulder and winced. "Don't know, sir."

From the curtained window looking out onto the dark street, Danny peered skeptically over his shoulder at his brother.

The telephone in the hallway rang. "I'll answer it," Betsy said, heading out the door. She returned a moment later. "It's Dr. Senter. He wants to know if you have room to handle some of the people burned in the tent fire."

"Tell him I can help." Willis turned wearily to Brad. "Well, you're all patched up, son. You'll heal right enough. Carry a few scars to remind you of Cripple Creek, though. When you get to Trinidad, find a doctor there to look you over and to take those stitches out when it's time."

"Yes, sir."

"When does your train leave?"

"Two-forty."

"Well, try and find a quiet place to rest till then." Willis removed a watch from his vest pocket. "You have a little more than four hours. You're welcome to wait in the parlor." He sighed. "It appears the missus and I will be up most the night."

"Thank you, but we'll go on down to the depot and wait there."

"Good enough."

Betsy came back, saying, "They're bringing five over right away."

"We better prepare some cots and throw a blanket over the sofa in the parlor, too—"

Brad and Danny made their way out the front door and in the cool, night air walked back down towards Bennett Avenue.

"I'm glad we're going to wait at the depot, Brad," Danny said. "I'm flat tired of this town. Sooner we're gone, the better I'm gonna like it."

"We ain't going to the depot," Brad said flatly.

Danny stopped. "But you told the doctor—"

"Never mind what I told him. I still got to find that one-eyed man and get my watch back."

"Maybe he didn't make it out of the fire, Brad."

Brad thought a moment. "We'll go back and see."

Danny shook his head.

"It's on the way to the depot anyway," Brad said.

"What will you do if he is dead?"

"I don't know. Maybe we can take the watch off his body."

"You can't do that, Brad."

"Why not?"

"Because there'll be folks watching. It ain't proper, stealing from a dead person."

"It ain't stealing!"

"Yes, it is. You lost your watch fair and straight and I wish you'd just forget about it."

"I'm going anyway—" Brad's words broke off suddenly when a hand came down on his shoulder. He turned, startled, and looked up into a weathered face he recognized instantly.

"The only place you're going is back to the police department—with me," Devon said, studying him in the glow of a gaslight. "Looks like the doc did a fair job of patching you up, son, and I'm going to see to it you stay that way."

"We'll go with you," Danny said eagerly, relieved to see Devon again.

"I ain't going." Brad took a firm stance.

Devon narrowed an eye at the boy. "You're tall for your age, son, but you're still a sapling as far as I can see, and trouble runs in your footsteps. I figure it's my duty as a public servant to get you off the streets and safely on the train out of town."

"I'm seventeen!" Brad said defiantly.

Devon grinned. "I'll be seventy-one come March. Someday, maybe, you'll be that old—maybe. What I've seen so far, I rather doubt it." He stopped, grinning. "I've got a son of my own and I wish to hell when he was seventeen I'd have taken a firm hand with him. He's forty-seven now. His ma died when he was seven and I wasn't enough of a man to be a father to him when he was growing up. I peddled him off from one kin to another until I ran out of kinfolk. Then I left him alone at a boarding house where I figured he'd be watched after while I went out taking care of what I *thought* was important business. All the time the *important* business was home, getting into trouble."

Devon paused, then said ruefully, "Well, I don't have to worry about watching over him now. He's in a Kansas state prison, doing life for armed robbery and murder."

Brad didn't reply.

"It's too late for him, but not for you. Now, you can come back with me of your free will or I can think up a charge or two to arrest you on. Maybe breaking curfew—or perhaps I can tie you two in with that tent fire tonight. . . ."

Brad looked up sharply.

Devon grinned again. "Your clothes smelled of smoke when I found you in the alley. It doesn't take a whole lot of brains to put two and two together."

Brad nodded his head with the bitter taste of defeat in his mouth. "We'll go with you," he said, but he knew there'd come that moment when no one would be watching. Then he and Danny would be gone, quick as lightning, and he'd find that one-eyed man—and his watch!

* * *

"I did it again. Made a mighty fool of myself in front of God knows how many people, didn't I, girlie?" Grace DeVere smacked her parched lips, trying to work moisture into them; they felt like starched linen.

Crystal gently ran her fingers through the old woman's tangled gray hair. "It's all right now. You had a bad time of it, but that's over."

Grace looked down at herself, aware of a dull pain behind her eyes. "Who took my clothes off?"

"You did."

She managed a bemused smile. "You saying I pranced around in my birthday suit?"

"You drew quite a crowd from what Mr. Kraker tells me."

"He put this blanket about me?"

"Yes."

"He's quite the gentleman, ain't he."

"I think so." Crystal glanced over at the tired old man sitting behind the desk across the room.

Grace looked at the jail as if suddenly aware of her surroundings. "I've been here before," she commented unemotionally. "Starting to look like a second home to me."

"It's the opium, Grace, and your drinking." Crystal adjusted the blanket up around Grace's shoulders. "They will be the death of you."

"And if I quit them, life will be the death of me."

"Don't talk like that."

"It's true," she replied softly. "I'd have been better off—the world would have been better off—if I'd just never woke up."

"Hush."

"Don't hush me, girlie! I know what I'm saying. And don't think I haven't given it some serious thought. I was thinking about it when I opened the bottle this evening. I'm still thinking about it. What's left for me? What will be left for you, Crystal, in twenty-five more years, if you live that long? You get old, you lose your figure. Men won't come around no more then. What do you have in the world left but a few lousy memories and the battle scars from a thousand different men. You know what I'm talking about, girlie. You already carry some—" Grace moved aside the blanket and revealed a portion of her flabby stomach. Her finger traced the white, gnarled line of an old scar. It crisscrossed her belly and made an irregular line up the center of her torso, ending six inches below her neck.

"A bastard named J. D. Carpenter made me a present of this more than twenty years ago. It's an unsightly reminder of what our kind of work can do to a girl."

Crystal swallowed down an ill feeling and moved the blanket back in place. "I never knew, Grace."

"Of course you didn't, girlie," she replied bitterly. "It ain't something I'm proud to show off. I reckon the whole town knows now," she added softly, as if speaking only to herself.

Crystal thought of the scars she too carried and that she was only nineteen years old. The age of forty-five was unfathomable, and suddenly terribly frightening.

"But you're all right now." Crystal tried to sound comforting.

Grace withdrew into herself. "I will be soon," she replied distantly, her mind suddenly somewhere else.

"Can I get you anything, Grace?"

Grace's tired, yellowed eyes moved in their sockets. "I sure would appreciate a glass of water, if you don't mind."

"Of course." Crystal stood and concern pulled down at

the corners of her mouth. Grace stared into space, moving her parched lips in an unconscious manner.

"How is she?" Kraker asked.

Crystal went to his desk. "I don't know. Depressed. Very depressed. I was just getting her a glass of water—"

"After that drug and the whiskey, I reckon her tongue must feel like the floor of a saloon."

"She needs a good night's sleep."

"Is she well enough to go home?"

Crystal thought a moment. "I'd say yes, but I think she would be better off here for the night where someone can keep an eye on her."

Kraker nodded his head. "That was my feeling, too."

Crystal returned with the glass. Grace was sitting up on the cot.

"Thank you, girlie," she drank ravenously, emptied the glass and dabbed her lips with the corner of the blanket.

"I'm sure a sight, ain't I?"

"I've seen you in better times," Crystal replied with a forced smile.

"I suppose I ought to make myself decent." Grace adjusted the blanket over her shoulders. "I don't want to walk back to my place dressed in nothing but a blanket."

"Grace," Crystal said, "I think Ben Kraker is going to keep you here for the night."

"Oh?" Grace withdrew a moment into her thoughts, then her face brightened. "I still can't spend the night with no more than a blanket, girlie. Suppose you do me a favor and run down to my shop. I've some clothes laid out up in my room. You can bring them to me?"

"Certainly, and anything else you'd like."

"Well, maybe you can bring along my purse, too. I've some things in it I can use," she said, flattening her eyebrows with a moist finger.

"Of course, I'll be back in a little bit," she said.

"Lock the place, too, when you finish," Grace added, as Crystal started for the door.

"I'm going to fetch Grace's clothes," Crystal informed

Ben Kraker, stopping momentarily at his desk. "I think she's feeling better."

"Glad to hear that. I don't much care to keep a lady locked up. If she's feeling right enough, she can have my bed upstairs. I won't be using it tonight."

"That will be nice; I'll let her know." Crystal left as Walt Devon came in with Brad and Danny. She paused, looking at Brad. "Are you feeling better?"

"Yes, ma'am," he answered, his eyes glancing away from her, embarrassed that she should see him like that, an embarrassment Crystal sensed and understood.

Crystal said, "I need to run off and get a few things for Grace. Perhaps I will see you later." She gave Devon a knowing glance and hurried out the door.

"You look a sight better than the last time I saw you," Kraker noted, and said to Devon, "You and the boys make another turn through the town?"

"I found them out wandering around. I figured I needed to make this town safe again, so I hauled them in. They're riding out on the train tonight with me. I told them they could wait here."

"Why not," Kraker said. "Might as well fill the building when we can. It will sort of make up for those long nights when I sit here alone." He chuckled. "After tonight I'll appreciate the quiet times."

Devon nodded at the line of cells. "How is she?"

"Tired, depressed, cottonmouthed." Kraker shrugged his shoulders. "About what you would expect."

"And him?"

"Unusually quiet. I think he's considering what you said. Maybe he's finally getting worried. Maybe big brother Bernard isn't going to pull his fat from the fire this time."

Devon removed his hat and shook his head. "I'd like to believe that."

"You don't?"

Devon didn't know what he believed. He looked at the cell that now contained three men and thought of the long, dark street with its dark buildings and rooftops and alleyways. It was all too perfect. Maybe it was the weight of his years, pressing down upon him, making him edgy. He hung his hat on the hook and draped the gun belt after it.

"Remember the time those Blackfeet wanted our winter's catch, Ben?"

"Hu-huh. You offered to take on the leader hand-to-hand with your Green River. If you won, we were to take their horses. If they won, they got our pack mules with the pelts."

"What did you think, then?"

"I thought you were crazy. That Blackfoot buck was near as big as you with muscles across his shoulders like the iron bands around a whiskey keg. But I was too busy holding your rifle and mine and keeping an eye on the other four to do much thinking."

"Remember what happened?"

Ben Kraker smiled, remembering back all those years. His gray head shook. "We were sure young and crazy, weren't we, Walt? Why, I remember it like it was yesterday. You laid into that Injun like a railway locomotive. He never expected a white man to have your leather. He figured you as an easy way to our animals and pelts. You sure showed him your colors that day. You chewed him up and spit him back out to his friends. We didn't take their horses either as I recollect."

"And we never had trouble with Bugs Boys again," Devon added.

"No, they did seem to cut us a wide swath after that. What brought that up, Walt?"

Devon thought a moment. "I have a notion we'll be facing Bugs Boys again, Ben." He nodded towards the cell and lowered his voice. "And when we do somebody is going to get chewed up and spit out."

He thought again.

"I only hope it won't be us."

NINETEEN

GRACE'S ROOMS were a sight. Unlike the tidy shop downstairs, always neat and presentable to the public eye, where she lived was a mess. How like the woman's life, Crystal thought, as she looked around the bedroom. An open bottle of whiskey stood on the dresser. The bedspread was crumpled and pulled back.

How like *her* own life, she thought ruefully. All peaches and cream on the outside, cobwebs and dust on the inside. I'm being melancholy now. I'm only tired, she told herself.

Crystal nudged a pile of dirty clothes with the toe of her shoe, then spied a purple dress draped over the back of a chair. In a drawer she located underwear and hose. Shoes, a hat, a shawl—she discovered two empty whiskey bottles in her search and shut a window that was letting in chilly night air.

Crystal put it all into a shopping bag she found in Grace's wardrobe, then looked around for the purse. It turned up wedged between the bed and the dresser.

"Oh my." She strained, lifting it. "What on earth does she keep in here?" she wondered aloud. *Some things in it I can use.* "I'll bet," Crystal mused, hauling the purse and the bag of Grace's clothing down the steps. She locked the door on her way out and added the weight of the key ring to the contents of the purse.

Few people remained on the sidewalk, at least up on Bennett Avenue. One street down though Myers Avenue was still going strong and the sound of piano-playing wafted up to her on the night breeze. Thoughts of The Old Homestead came to her and she discovered, to her surprise, that she was quite happy not to have to be there this evening. Just being near when Grace needed her seemed to fill a void within her heart—that was funny. She'd never noticed that void before. . . .

* * *

Deirdre Ross paused in her reading. The story released her mind of its burdens—if only temporarily—and the weariness of the long day past crept over her now, but she fought it off, taking the remaining pages between her thumb and forefinger, seeing the thin sheaf yet to be read. She couldn't leave the story now. What was this intriguing Palace of Green Porcelain Mr. Wells was about to show her?

She stretched in the straight-back chair and adjusted the wick of the lamp, which had burned low. Opening the book again, her eyes were drawn to the solitary figure trudging up the street, carrying a bag in each hand. The woman climbed the hill and receded into the shadows.

Dismissing the lone figure, her eyes swept back, briefly coming to a halt on the masonry railing that stretched along the flat roof of the Weinberg Building across the street. Through the carved spindles, beyond the gothic tower, the moon was a pale glow behind drifting clouds. The clouds broke, moonlight reflected off the stone railing, then died and another cloud moved across.

She sighed. How ordinary life had become. How uninspiring. Charlie wondered how she could bury herself so completely in books. All he had to do was look around him and he'd know! But Charlie seldom looked beyond the front door of their cafe. How could she explain the other world she found between the covers of a book? A world she wished, at times, she could escape into and never return from.

That line of thought reminded her of the reason she couldn't sleep in the first place. She would have none of that now—not when there was another world waiting to take her away from it all. She opened the book, and closed out everything else.

* * *

Brad sat on the bench against a far wall where Devon had placed him, arms folded, a storm-cloud scowl on his face. Beside him Danny flipped through a book Ben Kraker had handed him when he noticed the boy fidgeting in his seat. The words meant little, but the line-cut drawings were intriguing and he rotated the book to view them from different angles.

"We got to figure a way out of here, Danny," Brad said in a low voice.

Danny pretended not to hear.

Across the room Ben Kraker dozed in his chair. Brad watched Devon running a cleaning rod through the opened breech of a double-barreled shotgun. Milo Johnson was still struggling with his type-writing machine and Kern McDonald and Frank Sayers were fussing over scattered papers on their desks. The occupants of the jail cells were quiet, Grace DeVere appeared to be asleep.

The door opened and Crystal came in, hauling her heavy bundles, startling Ben awake.

"I'll help you with that," Devon offered.

"Thank you, marshal." She smiled at Brad.

A rush of color flooded his face and he looked quickly down at the floor, but stole a glance as she turned away and went to Grace. The older woman rolled on the cot and adjusted the blanket.

"Oh, you're back. I must have dozed."

Crystal helped her sit up. "I brought the things you asked for," she said gently brushing aside the strands of hair that fell across Grace's eyes.

"You locked the place up?" Grace asked sharply.

"Tight as a drum, Grace. Closed the upstairs windows, too."

Grace looked pleased, strangely content. "Good, that's good. Can't trust no one in this flea-bitten town, you know."

Crystal removed the dress from the bag and shook out the wrinkles. "Ready to get dressed?"

"I can't go out like this, now, can I?"

Crystal repressed a frown and wondered if Grace had forgotten she was spending the night here. "Ben says you can have his room upstairs for the night." She helped Grace to her feet. "You don't have to spend it down here in the jail."

Grace looked surprised and then suddenly pleased. "What a generous offer. Ben is a nice man when he doesn't let his job get in the way."

Crystal agreed and gathered Grace's things in her arms. "Ben, we need to use the closet," she said to him.

He motioned at the hallway beyond the cells. "It's just around the corner."

Brad watched the two women disappear down the hallway. He approached Ben Kraker. "The air is getting a bit stale in here, sir. Mind if my brother and I step out the door for a few minutes?"

"They're your prisoners, Walt," Kraker said with a grin.

"The air seems fine to me," Devon answered flatly.

"You have no right keeping us here."

"Perhaps not, son. If you feel inclined to file a complaint, here is the man to see."

"Now don't get me in the middle of this, Walt."

Crystal came back into the room. "Grace seems in better spirits," she said, stopping by the desk. "She asked to be alone. I think she wants to fix herself up before she's seen again. The poor thing."

"When she comes out, I'll take her up to my rooms," Ben offered.

"I'll stay with her a while longer." Crystal looked at Brad. "I must say, you're looking better."

"I'm feeling better, ma'am," he replied, and went back to the bench.

"What's the matter with him?" she asked softly.

"I'm not exactly sure," Devon said. "Something's unsettled the boy."

She thought she knew what had unsettled the boy . . . *the boy?* She smiled to herself. He didn't look like a boy to her, despite what the marshal thought. He looked good to her, maybe good enough to . . . she shook **the** crazy thoughts from her head. Crystal knew what she was, knew pretty much what her future would be. She had seen her future mirrored in the wrinkled faces and sagging bodies of the madames that had gone before her. She sometimes allowed herself sunny dreams, but life's reality always hung like gathering storm clouds just over the horizon. She was too old to delude herself with little-girl fairy tales.

"Ben," she started to say, when the words caught in her throat. A muffled explosion turned all their heads at once towards the hallway.

Devon spun on his heels with the others following. He paused at the closet door, smelling the heavy odor of gunpowder. It was unlocked. He turned the handle and pushed it open a few inches, but something heavy on the floor stopped it. Ben, Crystal and Brad had piled into the narrow hallway behind him. "You two better wait out there," he said, knowing what he was going to find beyond the door.

"No!" Crystal said, startled. "Grace is my friend!"

"Open it, Walt," Kraker said.

Devon pushed the door open.

"My God," Crystal cried.

Kraker frowned, turned to Milo Johnson. "Get the coroner on the phone."

Danny had wormed his way between them and now he felt suddenly sick. He wiggled back out into the hallway and sat down in a chair.

Devon removed the gun from her fingers. "A .44 Lightning," he said, looking at the heavy gun.

Kraker made a face and shook his head. "Why did she do it?" He sighed heavily. "Where the hell did she get the gun from, anyway?"

Crystal peered up from the floor where she had knelt involuntarily, tears gathering in her eyes. "I must have brought it, Ben. It must have been in Grace's purse. I thought it felt awfully heavy." She looked back at Grace, closed her eyes and suddenly her head was reeling. She was aware of a pair of strong hands helping her off the floor. She allowed herself to be led from the hallway. In the main room she was guided to a chair.

"Thank you," Crystal said, then saw with surprise that it was Brad who had helped her.

Brad stood for a long moment, looking down at her. He ached to hold her, to comfort her, and himself—but something drove him away. He glanced at the hallway, heard Kraker and Devon speaking in hushed tones. Now was his chance. If he was ever going to get away and find that one-eyed man and get his watch back, it was now. He tried to put out of mind the vision of Grace DeVere lying in a pool of her own blood, the splattering of red across the walls, the sink and the white porcelain toilet. He calmed an uneasiness that churned in his stomach and turned away from Crystal.

"Where are you going?" she asked.

"Come on," he said to Danny, ignoring her and taking his brother's hand. "Let's get out of here."

"But . . ." Danny tried to protest, unsuccessfully. Brad pulled him from the chair and out the door.

TWENTY

A CHARRED, smoldering circle was all that remained. The people were gone, the pumper returned to the station, the injured and dead carted off to their respective destinations—the morgue or various doctors' homes around town. A hospital was being built, but it would be another year before it would be finished. Brad and Danny stood alone in the dark among the heavy odors of wet ashes and the sulfur smell of a sleeping-dragon locomotive waiting at the station.

"That one-eyed man ain't here, Brad."

"I know," he answered wearily.

Danny glanced at the depot. "You better take it easy, like the doctor said."

"I'm all right." He touched the bandages under his chin. With each movement of his head, his wounds ached like fire, but he didn't let it show.

Danny shivered in the night air. "What are we gonna do now?"

Brad scuffed to the sidewalk and sat down, while Danny peered into a darkened store window.

"There is only one place I can think of to look. If he ain't there, well, maybe we'll come back here and wait for the train."

"You mean you'd give up?"

Brad looked at him. What was it he saw in his brother's face? Surprise or relief? "I'm tired," he said flatly, realizing it now for the first time as he sat there with the lateness of the hour and fullness of the day a growing burden upon him.

Danny sat next to him. "You think maybe he's back at that saloon?"

"There, or one of the others. We can at least look 'em over, don't you think?"

"I think so, Brad."

Brad regarded his brother thoughtfully. He didn't understand this sudden acquiescence. He stood and his body ached all over.

They went down the hill to Myers Avenue, into a flood of people and noise that anesthetized the pain, numbing his senses. They made a quick turn through the first five saloons on the upper end of Myers, then headed down into its heart. Brad paused for a long moment in front of The Old Homestead, bright and noisy, curtains drawn and lighted, displaying an endless pattern of moving shadows.

"We need to keep looking, Brad?"

"Huh? Oh, yeah." He moved under Danny's prompting, his eyes riveted upon that door. It had lost its foreboding magic, its titillating promise.

The next two saloons harbored no one-eyed man. The Union Theater had a line of men waiting outside to see Cleo the Egyptian Belly Dancer. He wasn't among them either. They tried the Opera Club, Last Chance, Swanee River, Old Yellowstone, and, swinging around to start back, poked their noses into another twenty barrooms with no luck.

"I think maybe he's not here anymore," Danny sighed.

Brad had to agree. "One more place, OK?"

"OK. Which one?"

Brad looked around. There were plenty to choose from. "That one," he said, for no particular reason except that it was closest, pointing at the Miners Exchange. They walked up to the batwings and into the smoky interior.

*   *   *

The coroner took Grace DeVere away. A heavy silence settled through the jail house. Devon poured himself coffee, offered a cup of it to Crystal.

"No, thank you." She realized that Ben Kraker was watching her from hooded eyes. "I didn't mean to bring it . . ." she started to say and her voice gave out under the strain.

"Of course not." He rose stiffly to his feet, put a comforting arm over her shoulder. "Nobody's blaming you."

"I know. Yet I feel so responsible. If I'd only looked in her handbag. It was so heavy, but I never imagined . . ."

"You couldn't have stopped her, not even if you'd found the gun. She would have found another way," Devon said.

"But why?"

"You really don't know?"

She looked at him, startled. "Should I?"

He thought a moment, then shook his head, recalling how long he'd lived before he learned the deceptive tricks life and a man's own ideas of importance and worth play on him. True, he'd been lucky at times. The incident with the Blackfeet when he and Kraker had been young and reckless and later, taking on a dozen cowmen to save Ben's neck from a rope. He succeeded then and a hundred times since. But when he failed, he failed big. Ferro had been a failure.

"I suppose not," he said.

She wiped her face. "I'd better go," she said standing.

"I'll walk you home," Kraker offered.

"No, thank you. I'll be all right. I need to think, to be alone for a while." She paused at the door, looked back at them. "Thank you," she said and was gone.

"Poor thing," Kraker said, easing himself into the chair.

"She'll make out all right," Devon replied, glancing over at the bench. "Damn!"

"What?"

"Those boys—they're gone."

"No telling where they are, Walt. Cripple Creek is an easy town to get lost in if you don't want to be found."

"I suppose I ought to stop worrying about them, Ben. They're not my responsibility."

"But you made them your responsibility. You know, Walt, if I didn't know different, I'd say you was trying ease your own conscience on Ferro with these kids."

Devon looked up sharply. But he knew Kraker was correct. He relaxed into a smile and shook his head. "Maybe you're right, Ben." He nodded his head towards the cell in the back. "I reckon I ought to be concentrating on that one and the reason I'm here. I got a job to do and it isn't baby sitting wet-behind-the-ears kids." He glanced at the clock. "Another hour. I think it's about time we bundle him up and take him out of here."

Kraker stood reluctantly. "I'll get him ready."

* * *

Karl Rheutters found Boyd Rawlin and told him how to locate Horschmann. Then he went round to the Miners Exchange to retrieve Bernard's rifle. He stopped for a drink and was just stepping away from the bar when he saw the batwings swing open.

"Well, well, well," he said. "If this ain't turning out to be my lucky day—"

"What's so damned lucky about it," the barkeep wanted to know, polishing the bartop with a dirty towel.

Rheutters jabbed a thumb towards the door. "Look what just come through."

He glanced at the kids. "So what?"

"So, they're gonna make me some points with you know who."

He stopped his circular movement with the towel. "Them's the kids Bernie's been looking for?"

"The very same." Rheutters worked the lever of the Winchester, chambering a shell. "I got me some collecting to do. See you later, Hank."

Hank grinned, showing a gold tooth. "Good hunting."

Rheutters signaled two men standing in the curling cigar smoke above a green-topped gaming table. They came together, then moved off in different directions, one taking a casual stance by the door. Karl and the other moved unseen through the crowd. Danny and Brad had only one object in mind in their search and it wasn't until the cold steel of the rifle barrel touched his neck that Brad knew he'd walked into a deadly snare. Danny struggled against the arms that encircled him, but in vain. No one seemed to care, or even notice, as the two boys were taken from the saloon.

Around back, Rheutters shoved Brad against the wall, the rifle barrel hovered in front of his face. "You try to get away, boy, and I'll plug you, understand?"

"Yes . . . yes, sir."

"Good." Rheutters said to the men who had assisted him, "I won't need you two anymore," and they took off.

"The three of us are gonna take us a little walk now," Rheutters said, looking at the bandages on Brad's face. "Someone done a fair job of patching you up, kid. I'd hate to undo that, but if either you or that little brat of a brother of yours decide you can get away from me," he hitched the rifle up to Brad's nose again, "I'll make certain the only help you ever get again is a one-way ride to the Pisgah Cemetery."

He hauled Brad away from the wall by the front of his shirt, indicated to Danny that he wanted him to walk in the lead. They followed an alley, then a deserted side street down to a foot path beat into the tall weeds. The land began to climb. They went over a ridge and down into a pale, moonlit mining camp.

"Bernie! Bernie!"

"Over here," came a voice in response.

"That way," Rheutters said to the boys, indicating the direction with the rifle.

A form stepped free of the shadows that clung to a tin shack. It watched the three of them approach. In the moonlight Brad recognized Bernard Horschmann and the other man who appeared at his side, too. There was also a short, heavy-set man there, but Brad had never seen him before.

"Where'd you find them?"

"They wandered into the Miners Exchange, just as convenient as if I'd sent for 'em! I figured I'd bring 'em on out for you, Bernie. Figured you could use some cheering up," Rheutters said.

Horschmann circled the boys, thinking. Coming back around, he tugged at the scar under his chin introspectively and allowed the shadow of a smile to nudge his cheeks apart. "We can use them."

"Use 'em?" Rheutters wondered.

"Yeah, as bait. Bait for the trap we'll spring on that marshal when he brings Harry out of the jail."

Stu Gardner said, "I don't know, Bernie. We're digging a pretty deep hole for ourselves as it is."

"Something on your mind, Gardner?" Horschmann asked.

"No." His resolve shrank. "I just don't want to spend the rest of my days behind bars, or end them too soon, stretching a rope."

"You worry too much, Gardner." Horschmann was smiling again, but the hardness in his eyes remained. "Just do what you're supposed to do and we will *all* get out of this clean." His eyes compressed then, ever so slightly. "But you screw up and you're liable to drag us all under. I won't tolerate that. Do I make myself clear?"

"Yeah, I hear you."

TWENTY-ONE

DEIRDRE ROSS closed the book upon her lap with a sigh and a vague notion of discontent. Was it the story's uncertain ending or something else? Although she tried not to think of it, her thoughts came back to the old marshal who had taken dinner in her cafe, and to Bernard Horschmann's stranglehold on the small businessmen of Cripple Creek. That line of thinking brought her back around to her father, the sort of man he was, the stark contrast between him and Charlie.

The discontent swelled.

She struggled to put her thoughts aside and blew out the flame of the lamp, but remained in her chair, in the darkness. The moonlit street showed the pitches and gothic ornamentations of the rooftops in a pale light that reminded her of the pale, chinless creatures that haunted the underworld of Mr. Wells's future—of death.

With a rustle of her robe she stood resolutely and lingered over the bed where Charlie breathed evenly beneath the warm comforter. No! She could not lie to herself! She was well-aware of what was keeping her awake. She looked at the clock. One-thirty. Softly, she padded to the wardrobe where she had left the door ajar. Moving aside her dresses, she lifted the old, brass-framed rifle out and set it gently upon the table. There was a box of shells on the shelf. She stretched for them, careful not to dislodge the other clutter there. She moved the lamp to the floor and muffling the metal of the rifle with the palm of her hand began to feed the cartridges into the magazine.

She had no clear idea of what she intended to do; that she was doing *something* was what mattered. She had been complacent too long. She loved Charlie, but she had not been raised to sit idly by and allow circumstances to ride roughshod over her. With renewed zeal she finished loading the Winchester and set it aside to wait for the time to pass. Bennett Avenue had finally closed down, but even through the window glass the sounds of Myers Avenue, two blocks off, came to her loud and boisterous. She blocked it out and remembered the silent prairieland of her childhood. A quiet imposed upon only by an occasional mournful bawl of a cow and the chatter of coyotes.

* * *

Milo Johnson came out of the hallway, set the bucket and brush on the floor and sat down on the bench where Brad and Danny had waited before the unpleasantness. His face had paled.

Ben Kraker glanced at him from where he stood by the rifle rack on the far wall. "You OK, Milo?" he asked, turning the key in the padlock and sliding the long chain from the trigger guards of the weapons there.

"I'm all right, Ben." He sucked in a deep breath. Color returned to his cheeks. "It was nasty business in there, but I got it all cleaned up."

Kraker removed three Winchesters and two side-by-sides. Dug out two boxes of shells and began loading the weapons. Milo said, "I'll dump this out back, Ben."

Ben grunted and continued working the shells into the magazines. Milo carried the bucket past Devon and Horschmann, as the handcuffs being snapped shut made a metallic click.

Devon turned Horschmann around, peered down at the younger man. "What are you grinning about?" he asked, noticing that Horschmann's two cellmates were watching with open interest.

"I'm thinking what a fine time I'll have spitting in your eye when you're laying dead in the street, marshal." His face showed a sneering confidence that made Devon wish he had been privy to what had transpired between the three of them while they had been locked up together. But experience had taught Devon not to put too much weight on the boastings of young fools like Harry Horschmann. Not to allow their chesty words to cloud his own clear thinking.

"Don't let him buffalo you, Walt," Kraker said. He held a rifle in one hand and a shotgun in the other. "Which one of these would you prefer to carry?"

"I'll take the scattergun, Ben, and don't worry. I've heard his words before, from bigger and stronger men than him. Hard-to-kill men." Devon eyed the short blue barrels of the shotgun with approval and said, "But I never knew a man who could dodge the buckshot from a twelve-gauger poked in his backside." He looked deliberately at Horschmann. "Have you, Harry?"

Horschmann scowled, glancing away. "I ain't afraid of you, marshal."

"From what I hear, that wouldn't be your first mistake, son, but it's liable to be your last."

A muffled chuckle came from the back cells, but Horschmann wasn't smiling.

Ben indicated the clock on the wall. "Two o'clock, Walt."

"We'll wait until two-fifteen. You better pass out those pieces now. Get your men together. Time to make plans."

When Milo came back, Kraker put a rifle in his hand and motioned for the others to gather around. Devon rested the butt of the shotgun upon Kraker's cluttered desk with a hand around the barrels. He looked them over, assessing each man's abilities through what he was able to detect in their different expressions. Milo Johnson seemed nervous, but that could be the effects of a weak stomach and a dirty job. Kern McDonald watched with intense blue eyes. Devon decided he was a man he wouldn't mind having cover his back. Frank Sayers stood with spread feet in a solid stance. His eyes were dark, and narrowed, and he held the shotgun in the crook of his arm in the manner of a man intimately familiar and comfortable with firearms.

Kraker looked weary with the color drawn from his

cheeks and his stance bent forward slightly at the waist. But his eyes shone with an alertness that made Devon see a much younger man—a boy astride a horse with a long-barreled rifle under each arm and those alert eyes darting between the enemy on the one side and himself on the other. How could so much time have fled by? It had been a different season then. It had been spring. Neither Ben nor he had reached their summer yet and now, here they were, after so many years of riding together and more years apart, both graying into the tail end of winter with the threat of a new spring coming on.

Devon buried the thought. He had a job to do and dwelling on the past wouldn't get it done. He said, "Both Ben and I expect trouble, although there has been no indication any is coming." He grinned. "Call it the premonitions of two old men. I hope it doesn't come. Nevertheless, we are going out of here with the idea it is. When we get to the depot, we can congratulate ourselves on how clever we were and you can all go home to your beds. In the meantime, we need to be aware of what we are doing and what is going on around us.

"We will stay on the sidewalk; that will give us cover from the rooftops on at least one side of the street. Johnson, since you have one of the rifles, you'll take the point. Stay about twenty yards ahead of us. Check each alley as you go past. Ben and I will be escorting the prisoner between us. Sayers and McDonald, you two keep to our rear. Sayers, you keep an eye peeled over your shoulder. McDonald, watch the roofline and the windows on the far side of the street. Any questions?"

There were none. Devon nodded at the clock. "It's about time. Let's get this over with."

* * *

Crystal Lane had no great desire to return to The Old Homestead. A feeling, she discovered, that surprised her. Until now, for the last year at least, The Old Homestead had been home to her. A pleasant life compared to what she had left behind in Leadville, but a hollow life she now suddenly realized. She thought of Grace, of her life—and death —and was caught in the grip of a violent shiver that had nothing to do with the chilly mountain air. There was no way to remove the woman from her thoughts now. As if the bullet that shattered Grace's skull also shattered the delicately contrived lie Crystal had built to comfort an otherwise lonely life.

Her footsteps, though unhurried, eventually brought her back. She stopped in front of The Old Homestead, peered sadly at the tall, brick building, adjusted the shawl around her shoulders and went inside. Hazel Vernon met her at the door and asked about Grace.

"She's dead," Crystal said flatly. She could find no other words to speak and hurried up the stairs to her room.

* * *

From her chair, Deirdre had a clear view of the street below—from rectangular roofline of the new police building at the far end of Bennett Avenue up to within a few buildings of where Bennett began. The Midland Depot was not visible but, if the marshal and Ben made it that far, they'd be beyond the range of her rifle and any aid she could render anyway.

She laid her hand upon the cold brass of the rifle where moonlight reflected off it and the white crocheted table cloth. Her plans had finally come together. She'd look for them coming up the street and only at the last possible moment would she dare raise the sash and sit ready if they needed help. She had been a fair shot as a youngster and she was confident she could, if need be, still hit a man-size target across the street or up or down it for several hundred feet. She had to be careful though. Careful to wait till the very last moment—careful not to wake Charlie when she raised the window—careful that when the shooting began she was sure of her target. Men hidden in shadows would be difficult to identify. She had to be very sure.

A flicker in the moonlight caught her eye. Deirdre leaned close to the window and studied the outlines of the rooftops across the street. All was quiet. Then a flurry of pigeons broke from their roost atop the Iland Building, clamored confused into the sky and fled away.

Deirdre watched the outline pressed against the moonlight and saw a shadow crouch across and climb to the adjoining roof of the Aspen Block. The shadow took on the shape of a man as it scurried up onto the next building, the Weinberg, and settled down among the turned spindles that made up the railing across its front.

Her heart raced and her fingers tightened about the rifle. She forced them apart and instructed herself to be patient. Quickly, she glanced down the street. Any moment she expected to see Ben and the marshal and Harry Horschmann appear. Behind her, Charlie snorted in his sleep and rolled heavily beneath the covers.

He settled down to rhythmic breathing. Deirdre returned her attention to the dark street, watching for Ben and the marshal.

It remained empty. She glanced to the top of the Weinberg Building. He was still there, now mostly hidden in the shadows, but she could still see him, and something else, too. The glint of moonlight off the rifle barrel that poked through the spindles.

TWENTY-TWO

CINDY RYAN had only recently taken notice of him and although she was much younger than he—twenty-one—she was not giggly or coy like other girls her age. She had accepted his invitation to the monthly Miners' Dance two Saturdays ago and he couldn't remember ever having a finer evening. She was warm, friendly, good-looking, with proper womanly values. And more than that, she liked him. Genuinely liked him, despite his short stature and the funny, shiny-billed cap he wore to hide his balding head.

He flung a stone and listened to it clatter down the pile of mine tailings that bulged darkly on the land like an ugly wart. He turned his head over his shoulder. Horschmann and Rheutters were making their plans. Boyd seemed anxious to nudge his way into the discussions, but he had been ordered, under life-threatening consequences, to keep guard over the two prisoners that Horschmann figured he'd bait the marshal with.

Gardner snatched another stone from the ground and flung it with undue forcefulness. It smacked off a rock like a rifle shot and Horschmann paused in his dialogue to look at him.

"Come over here, Gardner," Horschmann said, "I want you to hear this."

He shuffled across the open ground between them and buried his true feelings behind a neutral expression that he hoped came across as more a lack of interest than the true, gut-turning decisions he was wrestling with now. No matter which way he looked at it, one Harry Horschmann wasn't worth a dozen Cindy Ryans! And if there was one thing he was certain, it was that he didn't want to have to leave her on *his* account.

"Yeah?" Gardner shoved his hands into the pockets of his overalls. "What did you guys come up with?" he asked, sounding easy.

"Bernie here has got a humdinger of a plan," Rheutters said. "Tell him, Bernie."

Horschmann hunkered down and with a stick sketched the streets of Cripple Creek in the dust. "This is Bennett," he said, poking the stick in the ground between two parallel lines. "The police building down here, Midland Terminal up there." He drew two lines bisecting Bennett. "Third Street here, Second Street here. I'm figuring they will take Harry right down Bennett. It's the shortest, most direct way to the depot. Right at this point," he stabbed the ground at the corner of Third and Bennett, "I want you, Stu." He looked up at Gardner. "Since Roberts isn't here, I reckon you're the best shot with a rifle. You can climb to the roof of the Weinberg and have clear field of both Third and Bennett. I'll be depending on you to cover me when I make my move."

"When will that be?"

"When I get Harry away from that pesky marshal."

"What's to prevent him from stopping you, Bernie?"

"Rheutters here and Boyd. They will both be on Third, on opposite sides of Bennett. They'll be hiding in the stairwells there. When Kraker and the marshal pass Third, they'll leave the stairwells and move into position to set up a cross fire on Bennett."

"That's the good part. I like that," Rheutters said eagerly, sifting a handful of dust through his fingers.

"Don't get trigger-happy, either of you," Horschmann said, raising his voice so that Boyd could hear from his station overlooking the two boys. "I don't care about Kraker or any of his constables that may be with him. But I want to finish off that marshal myself. When you start shooting, hit him low. I want him alive. I want him to see who kills him. Hear me, Boyd?"

"I hear you, Bernie."

"OK. Now this is how it's gonna go. I'll wait till you and Boyd get into position. Stu will already be on top of the Weinberg Building. As soon as they walk Harry beyond Third Street, I'll come out of Second. I'll approach them with the two kids up front of my rifle. I'll demand a trade. The kids for Harry. The marshal will have to go for it. I think he has some kind of feelings for them. As soon as the trade is made and I have Harry, that's when I want you three to open fire." Horschmann lowered his voice. "When you do, Harry and I will hit the ground. I'll try for the marshal if he's still standing. Then I'll finish off that snotty-nose kid and his pint-size brother. If you three do your jobs, it should be all over by then. I'll make certain the marshal is dead and we can cut out."

"Cut out to where?" Gardner wanted to know.

"I rented a team and a wagon. They're at my place now. Rheutters will get it and bring it to the corner of Second and Bennett while you're getting in position on top of the Weinberg Building."

"Then where will we go?"

"I figure we'll head to Florissant, catch the Midland north and ride it to Hartsel. Beyond Hartsel is a post office stop called Haver. We'll leave the train there and take a wagon road that runs north to the C&S tracks. There we can hop the train to Fairplay. That should leave a cold trail for anyone following. Once in Fairplay we can catch our breath and make plans. Maybe cross the divide to Leadville, or follow the land over Fremont Pass to Breckenridge. I don't know. All kinds of possibilities once we get that far."

Horschmann stopped and eyed Gardner. "Something bothering you, Stu?"

"Huh?" The directness of the question startled him. Of course something was bothering him! The thought of leaving Cindy bothered him. The thought of leaving at all twisted his gut. But he kept that to himself and said, "Oh no, I was just thinking."

"About what?"

Gardner brought his initial startled reaction under control and said, "You're talking about a whole lot of hard driving, and jumping trains. Harry is gonna be wearing handcuffs. We're gonna have to figure a way to get those cuffs off him if you don't want to attract too much attention."

"He's right, Bernie," Rheutters said.

"OK. So we'll have to get the key before we leave. Either Kraker or the marshal will be carrying it. Probably the marshal. I'll make sure I get it. Anything else, Stu?" Horschmann asked pointedly, with a note of suspicion in his voice.

Gardner looked at the ground and fingered a pebble there, feeling the other man's eyes peering warily at him. "No, Bernie, I guess not."

"You aren't getting cold feet on me?"

Gardner's head came up with a snap. "No, Bernie."

Horschmann studied him a moment. Their eyes came together and Gardner looked away. "I'm counting on you, Gardner. You're an important part of the plan. Don't let me down."

"I ain't gonna let you down, Bernie," he said.

"Good." He grinned. "That's what I like to hear." He looked at his watch and pushed it back into his vest pocket. "It's nearly two already. Time to get moving. You give Boyd a hand, Stu."

"Right." Gardner stood, stretching a cramp from his leg, glad to be out from under Horschmann's penetrating eyes.

That left Horschmann and Rheutters alone. Horschmann took his arm and walked off a few steps. "When this is all over, Karl," he said softly, peering over his shoulder, "I think we ought to do something permanent about Gardner and Rawlin, don't you?"

Rheutters nodded his head. "You mean lighten our load?"

"Something like that. I don't trust Gardner anymore, and I never could rely on Rawlin. We can't leave 'em behind. They know too much. What do you think?"

Rheutters shoved his hands in his pockets as they strolled.

He said, "I think there is a lot of empty countryside between Cripple Creek and Florissant. Anything can happen."

"I think you are right, Karl. Anything can happen." He stopped and looked at Rheutters. "Why don't you make sure something *does* happen."

"Be happy to, Bernie."

Horschmann smiled. "It's a pleasure doing business with you, Karl."

TWENTY-THREE

KRAKER STOOD inside the doorway, looking back. The jail house was empty now, except for the two remaining prisoners secure behind iron bars—and it was quiet. Unusually quiet. The scrape of his boots on the floor, the heady odor of new-sawn pine . . . the quiet. Kraker fought back a shiver. It reminded him of a funeral parlor, and he was too old to be comfortable thinking on such things. He pulled the heavy door and turned the key in the lock.

The others were waiting for him outside on the sidewalk. "They'll keep till I can get back to them," Kraker said, sliding the key into his pocket.

Devon studied him with concern. "You all right, Ben?"

"There you go again. I'm fine, and the sooner I see the two of you pull away on that train, the better I'll be."

Devon leaned back, resting a hand on the butt of the pistol at his hip, looking narrowly at Ben Kraker from under the wide-brimmed hat. "I believe you as far as I can throw you, Ben."

"There was a time when you might have been able to pick me up and toss me a few feet." Ben shook his head. "But not anymore, Walt. So I reckon you're calling me a liar."

Devon gave him a smile. "I reckon so. You said something about sleeping in late tomorrow and then toting a pole down to the nearest water hole deep enough to hold a fish."

"That I did, and I fully intend to do so."

Devon said to Milo Johnson, "If you see Ben up before noon tomorrow, I want you personally to get on that fancy

Western Telephone Construction Company telephone of yours and ring me up at the penitentiary. Understand?"

"They ain't got the wires strung that far yet, marshal," Milo answered.

"Then use the telegraph. I'm gonna see to it that Ben takes a rest, even if I have to wrestle him down to the ground to do it."

Ben hitched the rifle up under his arm. "The longer you palaver, Walt, the longer you'll be keeping me from crawling into the warm bed upstairs. Let's get this yahoo down to the depot, so's I can call it a night."

Devon placed Horschmann between Kraker and himself. Harry wrenched himself free of Devon's grip and said, "You old fools, both of you. Neither one of you are gonna wake up tomorrow. Noon or otherwise. If you wake up at all, it'll be in hell—"

His words stopped short when the shotgun rammed his spine. "Then we'll be sure to invite you over for tea, young man," Devon said evenly. "Maybe a few hours in hell will sweeten your disposition some—as I said earlier, aren't many men who can dodge a scattergun at this short range. Try to keep that in mind if you should have the misfortune of seeing your brother somewhere between here and that train that will be waiting for us."

Devon motioned to Milo Johnson. "You can take the point now. Sayers, McDonald, you two keep your eyes open back there. OK?"

"Don't worry, marshal, we'll watch your backside."

Devon glanced sideways to Ben Kraker. "You ready, Ben?"

"Hell, let's get this over with. I fear you're getting wordy in your old age, Walt."

Devon allowed satisfaction to show on his face. "Age has its privileges."

* * *

Deirdre Ross kept the figure up on top of the Weinberg Building in view, glancing apprehensively from time to time down the street in the direction of the police building. The figure had settled down, presenting a well-defined silhouette against the waning light of a moon that was beginning to dip towards the horizon.

A movement down on the corner of Bennett and Third caught her eye. There, when she strained to separate form from shadow, was another man sidling up against the wall of the Weinberg, peering around the corner. *So*, she thought, *two of them*. She calculated the distance at no more than one hundred and fifty feet. Easy shooting for a girl who grew up shooting prairie dogs with an old Remington Creedmoor at two hundred yards!

She shifted her view back to the man lying in wait atop the building across the street. Occasionally, the pinkness of his face showed as he lifted it above the railing to study the street below him. Then he looked at her, and Deirdre's breath caught. But his head continued turning in the casual manner of a man generally surveying the lay of the land. He hadn't seen her sitting there in the darkness of her room and she breathed again, glancing down at the corner. The second fellow was still there.

Her hand came to rest again upon the rifle across the table. She recalled, momentarily, Charlie's insistence that they stay out of affairs that were none of their business. Was she being deceptive? There was already too much deception in her past; how could she add more and still conceal it? No, she thought, she was not being deceptive. This *was* their business. It was *she* who had told Rheutters the old marshal's plans. It was *their* cafe that had been victimized by Horschmann's tightening grip about the small establishments in town. *It was her business!* And besides, she told herself with some consolation, as soon as I squeeze off the first shot inside this little room, Charlie is going to know all about it. There will be no lie that will have to be concealed.

She brought her thoughts to a halt. There, at the end of the street, came the first sign of movement. A single man appeared, then, behind him, three abreast. She recognized Devon immediately. His tall, blocky form, taller than the others. And Ben Kraker, slightly bent and walking with a tired gait. She recognized Harry Horschmann, too, and as the company drew nearer she saw the stringers out behind with their weapons cradled in their arms.

The man atop the Weinberg had seen them, too. He ducked further behind the protecting coping along the top of the wall. The man on the street scurried across Third and down the steps of a stairwell there. *So, that's their plan.*

Deirdre unlocked the sash and raised it a foot. Cool evening wind ruffled the chintz curtains. She arranged herself behind the table, resting her elbows upon it as she shouldered the rifle. The moonlight picked out her target clearly for her; all she had to do was steady her sights upon it. *I'll wait, of course,* she told herself, *until he shoulders his rifle—just to be certain.*

She fixed him in her sights. An easy shot from this angle and small distance. She glanced down the street as the company of lawmen neared. Upon the roof, the man moved. Deirdre brought her eye back to the rifle, picked him up in the moonlight and brought her finger to the trigger.

A hand came down upon her shoulder. The rifle wrenched up and out of her grip. Deirdre turned around, startled.

"Charlie!"

"What do you think you're doing, Didi?" he demanded.

"Please, Charlie, don't stop me."

"I said, what are you doing—" Out the window he saw the party of men step across Third Street.

"That's the police chief!" he said, alarmed. "You weren't going to—"

"No, of course not. Look!"

Deirdre thrust her finger at the rooftop across the street. "It's him! Please, let me have the rifle."

"Didi," he said, realizing what was happening. "This is none of our affair. Come away from the window."

"No! No, I won't!"

She pulled free of his grip, threw up the sash as far as it would go and leaned out.

* * *

To Walt Devon the night had turned cold. He glanced over at his bent and gray friend and he thought of winter—a different sort of winter. The sort that descends on all men fortunate to cheat death long enough. It made him face his own mortality, something Devon seldom liked to do, especially when a challenge lay ahead—and, for some reason, he was certain one lay in wait somewhere along the long street before them.

That uneasy stirring within the depths of his brain, the tightness pulling across his shoulders, that sixth sense he never understood but always listened to . . . It was telling him to be wary now.

They started down the long, gentle grade into town. To his left and right buildings rose like dark sentinels to watch over them—and to hide danger, Devon mused. He removed the shotgun from Horschmann's back and cradled it in the crook of his arm.

"*You* all right?" Kraker asked.

"Huh?"

"You're tighter than a drum, Walt. Know something I don't?"

"I smell Bugs Boys, Ben. They're around and waiting, just like they were fifty years ago."

"Who the hell is Bugs?" Harry demanded.

Devon looked down at him. "Someone who's been causing trouble a lot longer than you—kin of yours, I should suspect."

Behind them McDonald said, "Ain't that a name the old timers gave the Blackfeet Indians?"

Kraker looked over his shoulder, amused. "Yep, that's what the 'old timers' used to call 'em."

"Why is that?"

"I'll explain it to you someday, when I got the time. For now you just keep your eyes on those rooftops."

Ahead, Johnson came to the first cross street. He paused, peered along its length from the quiet residential section to his left down to the bawdy tumult of Myers Avenue to his right.

Devon watched him start across. "All clear," he breathed softly to himself.

The greater length of Bennett Avenue still lay before them, but the Midland Terminal at its far end was distinctly visible with its outside lamps burning and the lantern of a locomotive, hidden on the tracks behind the tall building, burning a beam of white light along the right-of-way, illuminating white rock, making the shadows there stand out sharper and somehow unreal to Devon's eye. There was a time, he recalled, when lamps such as those existed only atop lighthouses perched on craggy coastlines. He'd grown old knowing only the pale, yellow light of a coal oil lamp or an open fire. The brightest nighttime light he'd ever seen until the recent installation of Edison's new electric bulb was a full moon in a clear mountaintop sky; his brain had not yet made the leap to modern technology.

They crossed another street without incident. Devon made a mental note of the rooftops and darkened windows as they went past. They had come to the center of town now. Johnson approached another cross street. He paused on the corner, saw nothing in either direction and went across.

Behind them Sayers said, "Open window, second floor, to the left."

"Merchant's Cafe," Ben replied. "I know the owner. It's OK."

They crossed Third. A moment later Devon saw movement ahead. He drew up short swinging the shotgun off his arm.

"Bugs Boys," Kraker said.

Devon went cold as the two boys walked stiffly towards them, Bernard Horschmann close behind.

Harry Horschmann jerked as Devon's shotgun buried itself in the base of his spine. "Remember what I told you," Devon said to him.

From the startled look on Horschmann's face, Devon deduced that the man would rather have faced prison than what was liable to happen next.

Sayers and McDonald bunched up. "Spread out," Devon said. "Give yourselves some room." They backed apart.

"What now?" Kraker asked softly.

"He's going to offer us a trade, I would say. Keep an eye out behind, Ben. I'll talk with him."

Bernard Horschmann stopped in the middle of the street. "Marshal," he called, "I want to talk."

"Well, let's see what brother Bernard wants, Harry." Devon moved him ahead warning, "Remember the scattergun, boy."

Harry nodded.

In the middle of the street, Devon brought Harry to a halt. "I got a shotgun in your brother's back, Horschmann."

Bernard looked over Brad's shoulder. "And I have a rifle in this one's back, marshal. I'd say we're even."

"Mister," Devon paced his words, "I'm coming through. Let those boys go and I'll overlook this. I'm not interested in you. I'm only interested in taking my prisoner with me. What do you say?"

"I'd say I'm not interested, marshal—how about talking a trade?"

"No good." Devon didn't know how far Horschmann would go, but he knew he couldn't risk Brad and Danny's lives. He wondered if Horschmann knew it, too. "I'll use this," Devon said, showing the shotgun. "Let the boys go."

"Not until you release Harry."

"You tell him, Harry. Tell him this shotgun is no bluff."

Harry's eyes moved nervously from the hard look in Devon's eyes to blue steel gripped purposefully in his hand. "He means it, Bernie. He'll do what he says!"

"And so will I, Harry."

"But I'm the one in the middle, Bernie! I'm the one that's gonna end up dead!"

"You tell him," Devon said. "It's up to you to convince him."

"Don't listen to him, Harry. He won't sacrifice these kids. Ain't that right, marshal?"

Kraker came alongside. "I think he means it, Walt. I think

he'll do what he threatens. He's kind of crazy from what I hear."

"Damn kids!" Devon said. "Why the hell didn't they stay put!"

"It's not their fault. You and I, we were like them, Walt. Too young to know danger till it rode right up to us. Too young to know we couldn't lick it—so we went out and licked it anyway. They are just like we were."

"You're probably right, Ben. I just can't help thinking that—"

"That that tall one could have been Ferro twenty years ago, and you weren't around to help when he needed it? Now you're trying to make up for that?"

In truth, Devon couldn't deny it. But it surprised him that Ben had read his motives so plainly when he had only recently discerned them for himself. Devon said, "I keep forgetting how well you know me."

Ben said, "So, what are we going to do?"

Devon turned back to Bernard Horschmann. "If you harm those boys, you'll never make it off the street alive."

"An empty threat, marshal. Maybe I'll be dead, but then so will these kids, and maybe you, too."

"You know I'll have to come after you."

"That's your choice, marshal."

"All right. I'll trade."

"That's sensible. This way no one gets hurt. You send Harry, I'll let the kids come to you."

"Both at the same time."

"OK with me." Horschmann gave Brad a shove. "Get moving, kid," he said, leveling the rifle at Brad's back.

Devon nudged Harry with the shotgun. "I'll be seeing you later," he told him.

Harry was smiling. "I told you, old man. I told you Bernie would win."

"That remains to be seen. Get moving."

Devon watched his prisoner walk away. Brad and Danny

passed Harry and approached him. He was aware of the
warnings going off inside his head, but he could do nothing
until the boys reached him, and safety—

And then the woman screamed!

TWENTY-FOUR

"BEN! It's a trap, Ben!"

Ben Kraker's head came around. Above the Merchant's Cafe Didi Ross was hanging half out the window, one hand gripping the frame, the other waving frantically in the air.

"It's a trap!" she was shouting over and over again.

Bernard Horschmann leaped for his brother and dragged him to the ground.

Devon's attention shifted to the two boys as the crack of a rifle shattered the tense stillness of the night. Instinct took over. Devon threw himself to the ground, grabbing the boys with him.

Another shot rang out from somewhere in the darkness. Devon saw Milo Johnson stagger back against a balcony upright and slide down to the sidewalk. Out the corner of his eye, Devon caught a glimpse of Ben dashing across the street. In the confusion, a dagger of orange flame stabbed out from the corner of the building at him.

Devon swung the shotgun, firing both barrels at once. Wood splintered from the corner of the building into the face of a gunman standing there. The man ducked back out of sight. From another direction a bullet kicked into the dust at Devon's feet. Devon glanced back and saw that Ben had made it to the cover of an inset door and was throwing lead at the corner.

Devon shifted his view in time to see Bernie Horschmann working the lever of the Winchester. He swung the shotgun around and tugged at the triggers, but nothing happened. In disgusted impatience with himself, he tossed the empty shotgun away and reached back for the pistol at his hip, but Horschmann already had him dead in his sights. Devon's hand halted and he could see the thin line of a grin spread across Horschmann's face, as he too realized he had gotten the drop on Devon. There was no need to rush it now. He took the extra moment fate had granted him to steady his sights on the old marshal.

Devon cast about for a means of escape. He readied himself to spring aside when suddenly from a darkened rooftop came a flash of orange and the sharp crack of a rifle shot. Horschmann lurched around. He stood there a moment, staring up at the Weinberg Building with wide, unbelieving eyes. Then the rifle slipped from his fingers and, like a marionette whose strings had been cut, he collapsed. A dark stain spread across the back of his shirt.

Devon glanced at the roofline, but he had no time to puzzle it out now. Whomever it was up there, he was grateful for the help. He palmed his revolver and fired two quick shots at the corners of buildings, where rifle fire lit up the dark street.

Sayers and McDonald were diving for cover. At that moment a bullet knocked Sayers's feet out from under him and he tumbled into the street.

Danny stuck his head up to look.

"Keep down, boy!" Devon barked, shoving the youngster's face back into the dirt. Devon scrambled to his feet. Rheutters came around the corner at that instant, swinging a rifle to his shoulder. Devon wheeled towards him and squeezed off a shot. Rheutters arched backwards and careened out into the street. The rifle in his hands fired once. A tongue of flame licked skyward and then the rifle disappeared into the shadows and Rheutters sprawled into the street, not a dozen feet from where Bernie Horschmann lay in the dust.

As swiftly as it had begun, it ended. The street was suddenly quiet and Devon wheeled around, trying to cover it from all angles at once. He went to Rheutters, turned him over with the toe of his boot and saw the wide, unblinking eyes staring up at him in death.

Another movement caught Devon's eye and he turned to see the younger Horschmann making fast tracks up the street. Devon raised his pistol and said, "Hold up, Horschmann!"

Harry came to an abrupt halt, his back suddenly rigid, as if at any moment he expected to feel the deadly impact of Devon's .44.

Devon caught him by the arm and hauled him back, pausing momentarily over Johnson. Johnson would not be calling him on the telephone tomorrow—or any other day, Devon regretted.

A voice called out from beyond the corner of one of the buildings. "I'm coming out! Don't shoot."

"Toss your gun away," Devon ordered.

A Winchester came cartwheeling through the air and landed in the street. A moment later Boyd Rawlin stepped tentatively out into the open with his arms stretched up above his head.

"Don't . . . don't shoot, marshal."

McDonald collected the rifle, and Rawlin, and escorted him to Devon.

"How's Sayers?" Devon asked when they came up.

"Flesh wound to the leg. He's OK."

"Johnson is dead," Devon said. Then he realized Ben was not around. He glanced to the doorway and saw the dark form laying in the shadows there. "Watch this one," he said, placing Harry Horschmann in McDonald's charge.

Devon's tired legs moved into a sprint. He was only distantly aware of the people even now beginning to gather at either end of the street, coming up in curious groups from down on Myers Avenue. Light behind darkened windows came on and heads in sleeping caps appeared at the windows.

He went to his knees beside Ben and turned him over. Ben opened his eyes and smiled faintly. "How'd we do, Walt?" he said with difficulty.

"We licked them, Ben. Just like the old days."

"Not quite like the old days, Walt—" He coughed and clutched at his chest. "I don't think I'm going to ride out with you this time—"

"Where'd you get it?" Devon asked, feeling for traces of blood.

"Don't bother looking, Walt. You don't think I'd let one of those yahoos put a bullet in me, do you? It's in here." He tapped his chest and tried to grin.

Devon studied him. "Your heart?"

Ben gave a short, pained laugh. "I've been living with this here broken-down ticker for years now. A fancy doctor in Denver told me I'd not make it this long." A coughing spasm drained color from his cheeks. "But I showed him."

For the first time that Walt Devon could remember, he felt helpless. "I didn't know, Ben."

"No one knew, Walt. How long do you think I'd keep this job if people knew I was walking around with a short-fused stick of dynamite in my chest—" Kraker's words failed and his lips curled in pain.

Devon put a hand under his head and laid it gently onto the sidewalk. "Anything I can do, Ben?"

Kraker shook his head. "You're doing it, Walt," he said. "Just waiting with me is enough." His words drifted off and after a moment his eyes fluttered and closed. It looked as if he might have fallen asleep, but Devon knew otherwise.

"Good-bye, old friend," he said softly, so that those gathering around would not hear. But he knew Ben had heard and that was all that mattered.

Then Doc Willis shouldered him aside. Devon stood back, knowing there was nothing left for him to do here. With a new heaviness in his steps, he walked back to where the boys were standing. "You two all right?"

"Yes, sir," Danny said. Brad nodded his head. Danny said, "How is Mr. Kraker?"

Devon frowned. "Ben didn't make it."

"Oh," Danny said, uncertain what the proper words were that ought to be spoken at times like this.

Devon turned to Kern McDonald. "Think you can handle what's left here?"

"I think so, marshal. You go catch your train."

Devon glanced back to where Doc Willis was bent over Ben. "I'll be back for the funeral."

"You two were friends a long time?" McDonald asked.

Devon nodded his head wearily. He saw his own weariness reflected in the faces of the two boys standing beside him. "Yep, a long time."

"I'm truly sorry, marshal."

Devon looked at him, surprised. "Don't be sorry for me . . . or Ben. We had good lives. We grew old. Ben's time is over. I suspect mine will be, too, in the not too distant future. That's the cycle of things, McDonald." He put a hand on Danny's head. "It's the young ones like these that ought to be grieved for when they go. Like picking a flower just blooming through the melting snows of spring. You can be sorry for that, not the burning of the chaff at the end of the harvest."

McDonald frowned slightly and nodded his head. "I see what you're saying, marshal."

Devon looked at Brad. "You still have those train tickets?"

He dug two crumpled tickets from his pocket and held them up.

"Good. We better get to that train before it pulls out without us."

"See you around, marshal," McDonald said as they started towards the depot.

There was no fight left in Harry now as Devon took him by the arm. Harry Horschmann glanced one final time at his brother lying in the street, then followed compliantly.

As Devon started away, he remembered the gunshot that had come from the roof across the way. He turned to study the roof but saw no movement up there. Vaguely, he wondered who it had been that had lent a hand when he had most needed it. He wished to thank that person, but there was no time left in this night for that now. Slowly, with the weary strides of an old man who had seen too many summers and winters pass him by, he resumed the long walk to the train depot.

Then Danny slipped his hand into Devon's hand and, feeling the young flesh against his old leather skin, Devon suddenly felt young again. He squeezed the boy's hand and together they walked to the depot.

*   *   *

On top of the Weinberg Building, Stu Gardner sat back in the shadows and stared at the rifle in his hand. Below him he could see Devon's tired gait carrying him up the street with Harry Horschmann in custody. The bodies of Bernie Horschmann and Karl Rheutters were being dragged off the street, while handcuffs were snapped about Rawlin's wrists. Gardner looked at the Winchester again. He would have flung it away in disgust, but he knew the problem had not been with the gun. It had been something within himself. But what? He did not know and was only now beginning to understand what the final cost of it would be.

Rawlin was alive. Gardner knew Rawlin would tell them all about his part in the plan. Even though he himself had been the one to put a bullet in Bernie Horschmann, he was not free of him! He'd have to leave Cripple Creek after all, or lose his freedom behind bars.

He weighed the choices left him. If he stayed, he'd lose his freedom, and Cindy Ryan. If he fled, he'd lose Cindy anyway. The choice was painfully clear. While he was free, there was still a chance for him. Perhaps in another town . . . another state?

He left the rifle there atop the Weinberg Building, made his way across the rooftops, down the back side into an alleyway, and fled into the night.

*   *   *

She stopped at the bottom of the stairs and set her grip on the floor. The girls—those not working—gathered around her, giving their hugs and their wishes of good things to come. Crystal had been well-liked. She would be missed.

Hazel waited for the farewells to be said and eyes to be dried. She looked slightly tattered around the edges and her makeup was wearing thin, even as the night was wearing thin. Still, she presented the illusion of dignity, even if she was a bit gaudily put together.

Crystal saw the strained look on Hazel's face. She knew Hazel had purposely waited for the other girls to leave. Now she approached and took Crystal's hands in both of hers. "You certain this is what you want to do, honey?"

Crystal nodded, feeling the onrush of tears she desperately wanted to hold back. "Yes—yes it is, Hazel."

"You went through a lot today," Hazel said, not in a persuasive voice, but merely as a tired statement of fact. "You know, a good night's sleep might give you a different outlook."

Crystal smiled faintly and shook her head. "No, Hazel, I can't stay. You are right. Tomorrow everything will look different. Tomorrow Grace's suicide will only be a bad memory instead of the hard reality it is tonight. Tomorrow I'll look around and see my friends, I'll see The Old Homestead as a comfortable place to live—I'll see what I'm doing as a necessary part of life to stay here. No, Hazel, I can't afford to stay another night. If I do, I fear I'll never leave and in twenty years, or thirty, I'll end up just like Grace or like her sister, Pearl. I don't want that. I don't think I ever did. I guess, until tonight, I never really thought about it much." Crystal knew she was going to cry now. "But thank you for wanting me. Thank you for all you have given me."

"It was nothing, honey. We love you." She hugged Crystal and both women wept.

Once their eyes were dried and their noses wiped, Hazel said, "Well, I just wanted to let you know you were welcome to stay. I understand what goes through a girl's mind in our business. Don't think I didn't question it a time or two myself. Shoot, darling, I still wonder what it would have been like being married to one man, raising kids and having grandchildren. I admire you for what you're doing. I hope it works out for you."

Both women turned at the muffled sounds of gunshots coming from the next street over. Hazel frowned. The girls in the parlor looked at the back wall as if there was something to be seen there. In a minute the shooting ceased and Mary Towers came from the kitchen, saying she thought that the gunfire had come from up on Bennett Avenue.

Hazel drew in a long breath and shook her head. "I'm glad you're leaving, darling. This is a hell town and you deserve better. Where are you planning to go?"

Crystal lifted her grip from the floor. "I don't know. I haven't decided. The train is leaving at two-forty for Colorado Springs and I intend to be on it, and that's all I know. I'll decide where to go later."

"Two-forty? You better be off then," Hazel said, glancing at the clock and pulling a shawl over her shoulders. "I'll walk you to the depot."

"That isn't necessary."

"Give me that grip," Hazel said, taking it from Crystal's fingers. "I won't have you walking there alone after dark."

"You'll be walking back alone," Crystal pointed out.

"Who'd bother an old lady like me? I'll be back shortly," she said to the girls over her shoulder. The girls waved good-bye.

At the depot, Crystal bought a one-way ticket to Colorado Springs. By the Pullman's steps the two women hugged.

"I admire you, Crystal. I truly do," Hazel said.

"Stop that, Hazel. I don't want to cry again."

"Of course not, darling. Please write when you find what it is you're looking for."

"I will."

"Promise?"

"Promise."

Hazel took Crystal's hand and shoved something into her palm.

Crystal unfolded a hundred-dollar bill. "I can't take this," she said.

"Sure you can. You're going to need it. I want you to have it." Hazel hugged her again quickly as the porter took Crystal's grip. She followed him aboard, looking back as she entered the lighted car. Inside, she straightened her shoulders, straightened her hat, wiped her eyes and fixed a resolute smile upon her face. This was her choice—and she was going to be happy with it.

* * *

"Is it over?"

"Yes." Charlie looked down at the rifle in his hand, then back at Didi. "I'm sorry. But I didn't want us to get involved."

"It's all right," she said, forcing a smile to her face. It wrinkled her lips and pinched her eyes. Charlie thought she looked just fine. He put his arms out. She turned away from them.

"I said I was sorry."

"There wasn't much I could do to help anyway, I suppose," she said distantly.

"You're angry with me."

"At least I was able to call out a warning. At least I did that much."

"I admit it, Didi, I was wrong. Still you can't go shooting people from your bedroom window." He tried to sound practical about it.

"I didn't see Ben," she said, talking to the wall. "I hope Ben is all right."

"You're not listening to me, Didi."

"I'm going to visit Ben tomorrow. I think he must be a lonely man."

"Good. I'll come with you."

Didi turned and looked at him. "Why? You never liked him."

"I don't dislike him, Didi. I hardly know the man."

"I think I'll do that. I'll visit him tomorrow, and I'll bring him a basket of fried chicken. Ben likes fried chicken. He orders it a lot." She sat on the edge of the bed. "I didn't see him," she said worryingly. "I hope he's all right."

"Sure, he is. We'll visit him tomorrow. Just like you say."

"I'm tired, Charlie."

"Let's go to bed. You're all done in. Tomorrow is a new day."

She lay down, then quite suddenly sat up and looked at him. "Charlie, there's something I want to tell you."

Charlie bit down on his lower lip and felt a spider crawl up his spine. Something in her voice alerted him to what was going to follow, and he did not want to hear it. "Not now, Didi," he said, but the resolute shake of her head told him that this was not something that could be put off any longer.

"No, Charlie. I've kept this back long enough. I need to tell it now."

"You don't need to," he said gently, but Didi didn't seem to hear.

"I used to work for Grace DeVere," she said all at once. "I know what you thought of her, and I know what you think of the girls at The Old Homestead, but Grace took me in when I had nothing. She gave me a start. Maybe it wasn't the proper thing to do and, to think back on it now, I wish I'd have done otherwise, but I can't change what was. And I'm tired of living a lie. So, if you want to leave me, I'll understand. I won't hold you." She drew in a ragged breath and sat there with the look of stone to her face, only not quite. A small tremble at the corner of her mouth gave away the feelings pent up inside her.

Charlie remained motionless a long moment, then he said softly, "I know, Didi. I guess I've known for quite some time now."

"You have?" Her eyes grew large. "But—"

He raised a hand to stop her. "I ain't never told you because I didn't want to admit it to myself. I thought that, if I denied it long enough and hard enough, that that would change what was." He frowned. "But we can't change the past no matter how hard we deny it. And a past like yours is not a thing you can keep hidden for very long in a town like Cripple Creek."

"What are you going to do?" she asked cautiously.

He shrugged his shoulders. "What can I do? I love you, Didi."

Didi discovered that tears were suddenly streaming down her cheeks. Charlie came to her and took her into his arms, holding her tight.

"I love you, too, Charlie," she said through her sobs. He held her for a long while and gradually her trembling body stilled. She had fallen asleep on his shoulder. He laid her gently back upon the pillow and drew a blanket up over her. He returned the rifle to its place in the wardrobe and turned to look at his sleeping wife, surprised at the admiration he suddenly felt for her, not certain why he should be feeling it now.

TWENTY-FIVE

"TIRED, boy?"

Danny had taken the window seat beside Devon. Across from him, Brad occupied the other window seat. Danny looked away from the spectacle of lights that was Cripple Creek at almost three o'clock in the morning. He nodded his head. "Yes, sir."

Devon knew once the train got moving and the conductor turned down the lights that Danny, and most likely Brad, too, would be fast asleep. He thought of his own son, recalling how it was when Ferro had been a child who was tired but wouldn't sleep. A short ride in a buggy in his mother's arms would do the trick in no time. For some reason, the memory didn't hurt now. Devon wondered why and discovered he was looking at Danny.

He shifted his view to Brad. The boy had lost everything. His jacket, his grip filled with whatever belongings he had brought—almost his life. His pride, too, but age and experience would win that back for him in short time.

"Tired, son?"

Brad glanced up.

"It has been a long day," Devon said.

"Too long," Brad replied dolefully, then straightened up in his seat with a start and looked past Devon's shoulder.

Devon craned his neck around, shifting his view to the head of the car, at the same time checking that Harry Horschmann was still securely handcuffed to the bench across the aisle.

Crystal was coming up the aisle. She saw them and

touched the porter's arm when they came to the seats occupied by Devon and the two boys. He stopped for her.

"Won't you join us, Miss Lane?" Devon said, snatching his hat off his head.

"Thank you, but I wouldn't want to intrude."

"You wouldn't be intruding," Brad said, startled at the boldness in his voice.

Her smile glowed, like a lamp wick being turned up. "Thank you," she said to him, taking the seat beside him.

The porter slid Crystal's grip on the shelf over the seats. Devon reached up and deposited his hat beside it.

She touched the dirtied bandage under Brad's chin and asked if it hurt badly.

"Not much," he lied, but with conviction.

Inwardly, Devon smiled. "You leaving Cripple Creek too, Miss Lane?"

"Yes. It seemed the proper time to go."

"Where are you going?" Brad asked.

Crystal sighed and shook her head, dislodging a limp strand of hair, which she brushed aside with disregard. "I haven't decided. Anywhere that's away from here."

Brad started to say something, then stopped. He fidgeted in the seat, glanced at Danny and saw only a blank, sleepy-eyed face staring back at him. Brad mustered his courage and said, "I hear that Trinidad is a nice place," reddening some at his awkward invitation. "Danny and I are gonna be there all summer—at our Aunt Lucy's farm."

Watching them, Devon wished he were young again.

"What would I do there?" Crystal asked.

"Trinidad is a growing town, Miss Lane," Devon said. "I'm sure there are a number of jobs a woman could find."

Danny said, "Our uncle owns a pharmacy. Maybe he would give you a job."

"Yeah, we could ask," Brad said, warming to the notion.

Crystal thought it over, then nodded her head. "It wouldn't hurt to give it a try, I suppose. I have no place in particular in mind to go to and Trinidad sounds as good as any."

The train lurched forward and the lights of Cripple Creek slowly slid past the window, giving way to the darkness of the mountains and the glory of the starry heavens one only sees atop high mountains. The conductor came up the aisle, punching tickets.

Crystal and Brad were talking now, both excited about Trinidad—both excited for other reasons, too. Brad was a tall, good-looking boy—more than a boy. In some circles he'd be considered a man. When Devon had been seventeen, the trappers he hung with considered him a man. Looking at the two of them, he knew for certain that Crystal didn't view Brad as anything but a man.

Devon grinned, remembering something. He said to Brad, "What time you got, son?"

Brad's face suddenly saddened. Crystal saw it, too. "What's the matter?" she asked.

"I don't have a watch anymore. I . . . I lost it in a poker game. I . . . I was trying to win some money to—" He stopped speaking and the red returned to his cheeks, but Crystal knew why he had been looking for money.

"I'm sorry," she said softly.

Brad dropped his head and scratched at a spot on his trousers. "It belonged to my grandfather."

The air was suddenly filled with a light, metallic tinkling sound, playing the tune of "Yankee Doodle." Brad's head came up. Devon snapped the watch lid closed and the music stopped. "I ran across a one-eyed man who seemed hellbent on selling this here fine gold watch, so I bought it from him." He placed it in Brad's hand.

Brad looked at it a moment, then handed it back. "You bought it, it's yours. I lost it fair and square," he said, glancing at Danny.

"Now what would I do with such a fancy watch?" Devon said, frowning. "It belongs to you, Brad. It fits you. I've gotten along fine without a watch for almost seventy-one years now. I reckon I can manage the few years I have left without one."

"I'll pay you when I can."

Devon nodded his head. "You do that—when you can."

Brad slipped the watch into his pocket with a smile he could not contain. Crystal was smiling, too. The conductor came back down the aisle, turning down the lamps. Danny was already fast asleep.

In the darkness, Devon leaned back into his seat and allowed the sway of the car to lull him towards sleep. He needed it now—like he needed his daily nap these days, but that was a small price for growing old.

As he sat there, before sleep overtook him, he saw Brad reach into a pocket and extract the tattered newspaper clipping. In the darkness, Brad looked at it a long moment, then opened the coach window a crack and pushed the paper outside. It caught in the wind and fluttered away.

As Devon's eyes became heavy, he caught a glimpse of Crystal's hand moving into Brad's hand, and the startled look on the boy's face as he realized what had happened. Over the clickedy-clack of the wheels, Devon heard her say softly, "There might be a lovely view from the caboose. I hear tell one can see the glow of Cripple Creek's lights clear down the mountain to the town of Divide."

Brad gulped as Crystal stood. "But . . ." he stammered, "there ain't no caboose on the back of this train. Only a baggage car, and it'll be dark now. There ain't no windows in it."

"Are you sure?" she said, and the lilt in Crystal's voice even brought a blush to Devon's cheeks as he pretended to be asleep. "Come and show me," she said, all silky and warmlike, with her intentions not meant to be hidden now.

Brad stood, a little unsteadily. He attributed that to the swaying of the Pullman as he suddenly realized what those intentions were. He was grateful now for the turned-down lights that hid the scarlet glow in his cheeks. Without further comment, Crystal practically pulled him down the aisle towards the rear of the train.

Devon smiled to himself, recalling with a warm pleasure his first time with a woman. The boy would be doing some more growing up tonight. Then his thoughts turned to Ben

Kraker. He remembered the old days, the days of spring when they had been but children in the wilderness. Walt Devon still had his memories and, with his memories, he drifted off to sleep.

ABOUT THE AUTHOR

DOUGLAS HIRT was born in Illinois. He moved to Santa Fe, New Mexico, where he earned a Bachelor of Arts degree from the College of Santa Fe. Later he went on for a Master of Science degree in biology at Eastern New Mexico University, spending his summers doing environmental research work in the deserts of southern New Mexico, where, as he says, "I had to fend off roving bands of pack rats that nightly insisted on building their nests around the legs of my cot!"

Mr. Hirt now lives in Colorado, at the base of Pikes Peak, with his wife, Kathy, and their two children, Rebecca and Derick.